Emma:

May you [find in]
Hannah's Battle an arrow
or two of wisdom that will
help you win your battles.

Hannah's Battle

Best Wishes,

Blane Brummond

by
Blane J. Brummond

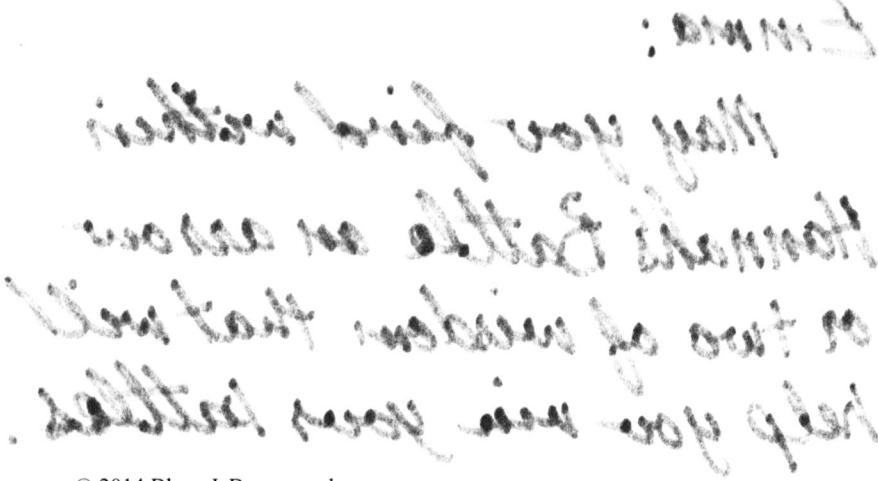

© 2014 Blane J. Brummond
All Rights Reserved.

No part of this publication may be reproduced, stored in a retrieval system, or transmitted, in any form or by any means, electronic, mechanical, photocopying, recording, or otherwise, without the written permission of the author.

First published by Dog Ear Publishing
4010 W. 86th Street, Ste H
Indianapolis, IN 46268
www.dogearpublishing.net

ISBN: 978-1-4575-2870-5

This book is printed on acid-free paper.

This book is a work of fiction. Events, and situations in this book are purely fictional and any resemblance to actual persons, living or dead, is coincidental.

Printed in the United States of America

Contents

Introduction		1
Chapter 1	Dark Trail	5
Chapter 2	Lost and Alone	8
Chapter 3	Brimble	11
Chapter 4	The Pool and the Pod	14
Chapter 5	Tough Choices	19
Chapter 6	Hannah's Dad	21
Chapter 7	The Spider Pool	23
Chapter 8	Misty's Thanks	27
Chapter 9	Misty's Mistake	30
Chapter 10	Hannah's Confession	37
Chapter 11	It's Not Fair	41
Chapter 12	Shaefrond	45
Chapter 13	Faisle's Report	49
Chapter 14	Call for Help	52
Chapter 15	Alone Again	56
Chapter 16	The Fey Host	60
Chapter 17	First Things First	65
Chapter 18	Michael's Cage	67
Chapter 19	Setting the Trap	70
Chapter 20	Ambush	73
Chapter 21	Verple's Contribution	78
Chapter 22	Trapped	83
Chapter 23	Nowhere to Run	89
Chapter 24	Tribute	93
Chapter 25	The Dimmenlarch Message	96

Introduction

The Fey have their ways. Even after years of observation and study, I still know only a small part of their world. Their customs, traditions, and behaviors are unfamiliar, to put it politely (as they would always have you put it), and downright strange, to put it another way. Some of their ways are clear and obvious, such as their reason for remaining hidden from humans and their fondness for remote and inaccessible parts of the world, and make perfect sense. After all, how could they get their business done if they were constantly dodging armies of fairy-seekers plodding through their wood, trying to capture the Fey and force them to grant wishes, give up their gold, or tell their secrets? Even so, most of what they do and why they do it remains a mystery to me.

 I have been able to learn some of the reasons behind certain of their habits through watching them or politely asking a question when no explanation was obvious. For instance, for a long time, I was curious as to why the Fey would sing before every meal. Finally, I asked a short brownie girl with silver glitter in her hair why they do this. The girl first looked at me like I was joking, and then, after she realized I really didn't know, rubbed her hands on her plaid skirt and took on the demeanor of a Sunday school teacher. "Don't *you* pray before you eat?"

Such was the way I learned most of what I know about the Fey. Still, many things about these mysterious folk, such as how they whisper the sickness out of plants or keep their gardens going all winter long, still baffles me. Please don't think I'm complaining. Even though I don't understand all there is to know about these curious folk, there is nothing quite so pleasant as opening one's milk box in the middle of January and finding it stuffed with freshly cut geraniums and the best-tasting cauliflower you've ever eaten.

Another matter that has always puzzled me is why the Fey chose me to write their story. Other than living a short distance from their wood, I had no special connection to their kind and had not done anything particularly notable that should bring me to their attention.

Still, choose me they did, and I have tried very hard not to disappoint them. I have kept true to their story as it was told to me but, on occasion, have taken certain liberties to fill in the gaps—and gaps there were, because the Fey see the world from a very different perspective than you and I, not just from being so short—below knee high to humans in most cases—but also from the things they consider important.

For instance, if one of the Fey were telling you about the time he rescued a kitten from drowning, he would start by telling you what the weather was like the year before the event and the effect that last year's frost had on his turnips. He would spend at least an hour telling you the condition of the bushes, the moisture level in the soil, and the particular shade of blue or brown the river water was the year the thing happened. Only after thoroughly describing the things in the world that truly mattered to him would he get around to telling you the thing you thought you were going to hear about in the first place. Then he might spend all of a minute on the event itself.

Because this story is not only of the Fey but also of a young girl with sky-blue eyes, a singing voice that could make a meadowlark jealous, and a quiet strength that would impress even the heroes among us, I have been forced to straddle a fence of sorts so that both stories are told. In doing so, I sincerely hope I have not annoyed the Fey, who, as I have told you, put great stock in long descriptions of humidity, soil conditions, and such things as the quality of tree bark. My guess is I won't know for sure until this winter when I check my milk box.

CHAPTER 1

DARK TRAIL

Hannah snugged a strip of tape around each pant leg, just above her hiking boots. It was something she always did to keep ticks and spiders from crawling up her legs. She could deal with most of the bugs that made their home in Ponca State Park, but not spiders. Spiders freaked her out.

"We'll fight this together, Sunshine," Dad said, shouldering his day pack. "Dr. Marino said diabetes is manageable."

"But it makes me feel like . . . like an *old* person." Hannah remembered that day at the doctor's office, the day her life had changed. *Diabetes.* She had prayed the earth would open up and swallow her.

"Not so, Hannah." Dad started down the path at a slow but steady pace in the direction of the morning sun just starting to creep over the steep hills. "Diabetes isn't just an old person's disease. People of any age can get it. The good news is it's manageable."

Hannah shuffled down the trail a few yards behind Dad. *There's that word again,* she thought, *"manageable."* "Manageable" in the case of diabetes meant sticking your finger five times a day to test your blood sugar, giving yourself shots, exercising regularly, and watching everything you ate or drank. *Yeah,* Hannah thought, keeping her eyes on the leaf-covered trail directly in front of her, *like a canoe with a hole in it is manageable so long as you keep scooping the water out of it.*

For a second, Hannah lifted her eyes from the trail to take in the beauty of the magnificent oak trees lining both sides of the path. Their gnarled branches resembled a thousand arms reaching in every direction. The oaks were home to a wide variety of colorful birds whose calls and chirps made the wood seem alive. Today, though, it was hard for Hannah to see the life and color the forest offered.

She and Dad came here often since Mom had left them. After all these years, Hannah could not say the word "died" when talking about Mom. She wondered if it would have been different if they had found her body. Mom and Dad had been caught in a freak landslide while camping in California. Dad had been knocked unconscious and awakened the next morning on a ledge 500 feet from where they'd been camping. They never found Mom.

Hannah kept staring at her boots as they shuffled along the dirt trail. There was so much to do here—camping, hiking, horseback riding, and, at the right time of year, mushroom hunting. The wood was wild, and the winding trail, birds, insects, and other forest creatures had a wonderful way of helping her forget her problems for a while. Today, though, this wood didn't seem to have the power to overcome the darkness creeping into her life. She barely noticed the giant trees or the heavy, sweet smell of the decomposing forest floor. The clucking and chirping of the starlings as they went about their courtships and nest-building was gone. Instead of a forest symphony, there was only silence—dead silence, except for the insistent thrumming of the awful word *diabetes* in the back of her mind. She heard nothing else, not even the sound of Dad's footsteps.

CHAPTER 2

LOST AND ALONE

A quick glance ahead showed no sign of Dad.

"Dad?" Hannah called in the direction she thought he should be. "Dad!" She cupped her hands around her mouth and yelled, "DAD!"

Dead silence. How long had it been since she had last seen him? Lost in her thoughts, she must have wandered down a stray path.

Fingers of fear clutched at her stomach. She turned and retraced her steps, calling for her dad every few steps. When she came to a fork, she couldn't remember which way to take, left or right, so she just picked one and ran until her throat burned and her lungs nearly burst out of her chest.

Finally, gasping for air, her face scratched from branches, she found herself in a small clearing filled with new quackgrass and a few snowberry bushes just starting to push out their tiny, deep green leaves. She knelt, her dirty jeans sinking into the soft grass, and began to sob. Before long, she was crying so hard, her body shook every time she took a breath. What had she ever done to deserve such a horrible fate? First, finding out she had diabetes and now, getting lost in the woods.

After a while, she wiped her eyes and leaned back, putting her hands on the soft new grass and dry, prickly leaves from the year before. She winced at the thought of poking her fingers to test her blood and sticking needles all over her body every day. She thought of one of her greatest fears: *What will my friends think of me?* She already knew the answer: *Weird.* Dora Sheckler already teased her because of the dark hair on her forearms. What nasty thing would Dora say when she saw Hannah testing her blood sugar levels? Hannah was sure no one, boy or girl, would want to be seen with her.

Worst of all, though, were the low blood sugars. She'd had two episodes since she'd started taking insulin. The first one had made her confused and shaky, and when she'd tried to walk to the kitchen, she'd staggered and bumped her ribs against the countertop. She shuddered to think of how Dora would laugh if that were to happen at school. The second episode had happened when Hanna had been taking a nap. Dad had tried to wake her but couldn't. He'd had to drive her to the hospital, where they had put an IV in her arm. When she had finally woke up, she'd felt terrible, like she'd run five miles up a hill with Dora Sheckler on her back.

Just then, a thought crept into her mind that made her stomach clench. *What would happen if my blood sugar went low here?* She had no sugar with her to bring it up—nothing at all, not even a candy bar. She didn't even have any way to check her blood. Dad had been wearing the kit with all of her supplies. She could be going low even now and she wouldn't even know it! The shock of the second worst week of her entire life fell on her like an avalanche. She remembered feeling like this only one other time: the day Dad had told her that Mom wouldn't be coming home. Why bother trying to save herself? If she didn't die in these woods, her diabetes would be waiting for her when she got out.

Finally, she decided if she was going to die, she didn't want to do it alone. She closed her eyes and prayed. She asked God to let Dad find her. She asked God even harder to take away her diabetes.

Nothing happened.

Eyes still squeezed tight, she held her breath for a bit and listened for the sound of Dad calling for her. Nothing. Nothing except the sound of the wind rustling the leaves right in front of her. *Wait a second,* she thought. *Leaves can't be rustling because . . . there is no wind.*

CHAPTER 3

BRIMBLE

Hannah opened her eyes to see that a bluebird had landed not more than two feet away. Its bright blue back, orange vest, and white beard reminded her of an old man who'd gotten dressed up for a fancy ball. She didn't know if it was his dressy feathers or his complete ignorance of her misery, but something about the little guy lifted her spirits.

"Hello, little fella," Hannah said, wiping her eyes and leaving dark smudges across her cheeks. "Thank you for letting me know I'm not *completely* alone."

In answer, the bluebird did a little dance. He kicked his legs and scratched at the ground like a chicken. Then he swished his tail back and forth and scooted through the grass in the direction of the setting sun.

Hannah had seen robins dance like this when she'd gotten too close to their nests. She knew birds did this to lead predators away from their nesting chicks. She wondered if the bluebird had a nest nearby. "Don't worry, little fella, I won't bother your nest," she said. "I have my own problems and don't see any reason for making any for you."

The bluebird kept dancing, no matter how much she tried to reassure him she was no threat. Finally, she followed the bluebird a short distance and let him "lead" her away from his nest. When she got to the edge of the clearing, she slumped down on a log and again thought about her miserable life. The bluebird twittered and cheeped at her and kept dancing into the woods. She ignored him—until he flew up, grabbed a tuft of her long brown hair in his feet, and gave it a good yank.

"Ouch!" Hannah tried to pull her hair away, wondering if there was something wrong with the bird. She'd heard raccoons and skunks sometimes had rabies, but she'd never heard of a bird with it. *Great,* she thought. *Not only am I lost and alone and will probably be dead by morning, now I'm being attacked by a rabid bluebird. What's next, a swarm of killer bees?*

The bluebird grabbed another tuft of her hair and yanked hard.

"Ouch!" She sprang off the log and took a step forward to lessen the pull on her scalp. This time, instead of letting go, the bluebird kept pulling her hair, fluttering its wings like a hummingbird. She took another step, and another, and another. Soon, she was walking through the forest on a small game trail, always toward the setting sun. Finally, the bluebird let go of her hair and flew in front of her a few feet.

"You really want me away from your nest, don't you," Hannah said. "OK, I'll play your game."

She ambled down the trail with the bluebird always leading the way. Whenever she stopped to catch her breath, the bluebird grasped her hair and pulled her along the trail. Finally, she found herself standing at the edge of a clearing.

The area was bordered by green ash and hackberry trees and was not much bigger than her front yard. The ground sloped downward from the trees on all sides to the center of the clearing a stone's throw from where Hannah stood.

"Oh my," she whispered, forgetting for a moment her own troubles. "What on earth happened here?"

CHAPTER 4

THE POOL AND THE POD

The ground was torn as if the earth had sneezed at this very spot. Scuffs covered the forest floor. Scratches were etched at the base of the trees where bark had been ripped off in great strips. Smaller ash trees and bushes had been completely uprooted and lay scattered around the opening, a few dangling in the lower branches at the edge of the clearing. Wet brown goo spotted the ground in places or hung in strings from the trees.

At the bottom of the slope was a pool of water that made Hannah suddenly realize how thirsty she was. It had been hours since she'd last drunk anything, and her tongue felt like it was glued to the roof of her mouth. She took a step closer to the small pond. The thought of getting a drink and relaxing for a bit made her want to run right down to the edge and jump in.

But something caught her eye.

Suspended above the middle of the pond was a pod, like a moth or butterfly cocoon, only much larger. It was about a foot long from top to bottom and widened at the middle, tapering off at the ends like a football. The pod was suspended at the top by a thin string stretched to a branch high in the forest canopy. The bottom of the pod was high enough that Hannah figured she probably wouldn't be able to touch it if she was standing on the surface of the pool underneath it.

I should get my drink before that thing falls in and ruins the whole pond, she thought. She stepped closer to the pond and peered into it. Little shimmers moved across the surface. *Good*, Hannah thought, *if this is coming from an underground spring, the water should be clean and cold*. She crept closer, keeping her eye on the pod to watch for any sign of it slipping into the pond.

Suddenly, the bluebird buzzed over her shoulder and perched on the pod. The bird started plucking at the pod, flapping its wings to stay in place.

"What a strange little bird you are," Hannah said as she came closer, keeping her eyes fixed on this peculiar show. The pod sagged under the bluebird's weight. The tiny string—spider silk, as it now appeared to her—seemed close to snapping. The thought of a spider spinning a pod that size sent shivery jolts across the back of her neck. As the thread grew thinner and the pod dropped closer to the water's surface, Hannah stumbled forward and knelt at the edge of the pond. She dipped her hand in the water—yes, it was cool—and cupped it, preparing to sip.

Something soft and hairy brushed her hand. Hannah jerked her hand out of the water. Something had crawled on her hand *under the surface of the water!* A groan emanated from the pod as the bluebird continued to peck it. She squinted, peering closer at the water, and froze.

Directly below the surface of the pool was a dark, leggy mass.

Spiders! What she had thought was water from an underground spring was actually a mass of spiders, spiders of all sorts and sizes, crawling upside down across the *underside* of the surface of the water. She tried to understand how these spiders could be underneath the water but still remain dry and very alive. It was as if the surface of the water was simply a thin lid, much like the plastic lids that covered food bowls at home, covering a container of air and spiders.

Hannah quickly decided she wasn't *that* thirsty. She leapt to her feet and headed back up the slope, wanting to put as much distance as possible between her and the spiders. She was halfway to the edge of the clearing when a small voice pierced the air.

"*Child.*" The voice was uncommon but sweet like honey dripping off a lilac bush, musical and full of color, like a bell made out of butterflies. "Please pardon my interruption, but if there is anything you can do to improve my condition before leaving, I would be most grateful."

Hannah whirled around in search of the owner of the voice but saw no one. "Hello?" she called to the clearing. She was startled by the strange and beautiful voice, but also thrilled that she was no longer alone.

"Hello," the voice tinkled.

It seemed to be coming from the spider pool.

Hannah decided it was only a trick to get her closer to the spiders. Well, she wasn't going to fall for it. But she was curious. She just wanted to find who was talking so she could assure herself she wasn't imagining things. As she was weighing her choices, the pod above the pool rotated on its strand of spider's silk.

A *face*! A tiny face appeared in the opening that the bluebird had pecked in the pod. It was a beautiful woman's face, and Hannah could see blond hair pulled back on the woman's head. Hannah took a step closer, careful to stay clear of the spider pool.

"Normally, it is not polite to stare," the tiny face said, "but, under the circumstances, I suppose it can be understood."

Hannah blinked and stood motionless, unable to make sense of what she saw. Her mom's mother, Volberg, or "Nanna V," as Hannah called her, had told her stories of the small folk that inhabited her native Norway, but Hannah had always thought they were just that, stories. She had never dreamed they were real. For a moment, as the face in the pod rotated out of her sight, she wondered if she had imagined it all. Maybe the diabetes was making her crazy. Great, something else for Dora to tease her about.

The face appeared again and said, "I believe a proper introduction is in order. Fellow traveler and visitor, I am known as Misty Meadowatcher, wood sprite, guardian of this wood."

The face did not speak again for several turns of the pod. Hannah's mind frantically scrambled for every scrap of story she'd ever heard about wood sprites.

Most of what she recalled came from stories told by Nanna V on the long afternoons when she visited with Hannah until Dad came home from work. Wood sprites loved and cared for the woods, of course. They were never seen in pairs. Unlike fairies, they had no wings and couldn't fly. They were known to have tempers and, when angered, could do a lot of damage.

She remembered one story about a friend of Nanna V's who had picked all the flowers in a meadow behind her house. The next day, she had awoke to find that all the clothes on her clothesline had been plucked off the line and thrown down the well. A note on the well had read, "Next time, please ask before picking my flowers." The note had been signed,

"Piny Petaltender." The woman had never picked another flower from that meadow. She remembered something else too. There was no better way to anger a wood sprite, Nanna V had cautioned, than to forget your manners.

With Nanna V's warning at the front of her mind, Hannah waited until the pod opening rotated to face her, then she curtsied as she'd seen in the movies. Mustering her most polite voice and lowering her eyes, for staring would be rude, Hannah said, "Good lady of the wood, I am honored to meet you. My name is Hannah Biel, but my friends call me Hannah." She glanced up in time to see a smile crease the wood sprite's face.

CHAPTER 5

TOUGH CHOICES

"As you can see, new friend, my situation is most unpleasant. I was wondering if you would be so kind as to see if there is any way to release me from this prison." Misty gestured with her head toward the spiders below her.

While Misty was speaking, the spider strand suspending her stretched impossibly thin so that the bottom of the pod almost touched the surface of the water. Once the spider strand could no longer hold the weight of the pod and the wood sprite, Misty would surely be captured by the spiders—maybe eaten! Hannah racked her brain for a solution. The pod was well out of her reach, but maybe if she had a long stick, she could bat the pod away from the pool. She raced to the edge of the clearing to find a stick.

In the damaged underbrush, she found a broken branch that would suit her purpose. She ran back to the edge of the pool and gasped. The bottom of the pod now touched the water. Her plan would not work. If she tried to bat the pod, which was no longer freely swinging, the bottom would drag on the surface of the water, the strand would break, and the pod would plunge straight into the pool. She winced as she thought of the wood sprite's gruesome fate once she was submerged.

Hannah tried to nudge the pod to the edge of the pool, but as soon as she touched it with the tip of the branch, it sunk another inch into the water. The spiders skittered and roiled in a great black mass, frenzied by the tip of the pod that was now within their grasp.

"What can I do?" Hannah cried out.

A look of sorrow came over Misty's face, and the music left her voice. "I know not, my new friend Hannah. However, there is a favor I would ask of you when this day is over. There is one who lives near the bridge where the fairies dance . . ."

Hannah heard no more as her only option became clear to her. Hands shaking, she tucked her shirt into her pants and walked to the edge of the spider pool.

CHAPTER 6

HANNAH'S DAD

"Geez, Michael, what the heck were you thinking?" Dad muttered under his breath as he slid down the stream bank and dunked his entire face in the cool water. It eased the burn in his throat from yelling Hannah's name to the woods for over an hour but did nothing to ease his aching heart.

He'd lost her.

Why, he asked himself for the thousandth time since turning around and seeing that she was no longer behind him, hadn't he let her walk in front of him? That would have been such an easy thing to do and would have let him keep a better eye on her. Now she was out in the woods, with darkness quickly approaching, without any water and without her diabetes supplies.

Michael fingered the pouch strapped to his belt. At a brisk pace, he headed along the edge of the creek, looking for tracks.

Diabetes was a serious illness, but, thank God, it was one that could be managed with insulin, diet, and exercise. He personally knew several successful people with diabetes, not to mention all the famous people such as Thomas Edison, Halle Barry, and Bret Michaels. People with diabetes have distinguished themselves in music, dance, science, art, and sports. In fact, it was hard to find any area of life where a diabetic wasn't making a significant contribution—but no matter how hard he tried, he had failed to convince Hannah that her life still had as much meaning and purpose as before she had been diagnosed.

She had been so depressed that he worried he would lose his Sunshine. That's what he'd called her since she was born. From that day, she had been able to brighten his darkest days. No matter how late he had to work, she always waited for him so they could eat supper together. After eating, they would pile the dishes in the sink and talk about their day or, once a week, take turns telling stories. She loved to sing, and sometimes while he drank his coffee, she'd serenade him with whatever she'd practiced in choir class that day. She had a beautiful voice, and he encouraged her to sing whenever the mood struck her.

"I don't pretend to know the mind of God," he told her, "but I'm pretty sure He didn't give you the voice of an angel just so He could hear you use it in the shower."

"*What do you sssearch for, humannnn?*" The hissing rasp of a voice came from the far side of the stream. Instantly, Michael's stomach knotted. Something was wrong, very wrong. He felt as if the world had suddenly filled with misery and everything good had been covered by a cloud. He could see something dark and huge twitch in the reflection of the water, but whatever was casting the reflection was hidden by a bend in the stream. Instinctively, Michael's hand grasped the end of a three-foot hunk of driftwood that could serve as a club if he needed it.

Five seconds later, he needed it.

CHAPTER 7

THE SPIDER POOL

Hannah's first step into the spider pool put the water "lid" up to her knee. She felt a sickening squish when her boot sank into the soft goop of spider bodies on the bottom. She kept watching Misty, whose eyes widened in disbelief. Hannah took another step into the pool, sinking to her upper thighs. So far, the tape around her ankles had worked to keep the spiders from crawling up her pant legs.

The disgusting feeling of countless pairs of mandibles pinching her thick jeans made Hannah look down. Big mistake. The moment she did, she froze. Both legs were covered with layers of spiders so dense that it looked like she was wearing a puffy pair of black snow pants.

Try as she might, she could not take another step. She was so terrified, it felt as if her feet were glued to the floor of the pit. She knew it was only a matter of time before the spiders found their way to her skin.

Just when it seemed she would stand rooted in that hideous spider pool forever, a note penetrated the paralyzing fear. The note, pure and sweet, hung on the air with a gentle kindness that seemed incompatible with this place. Like water and fire or baby laughter and sadness, they could not live in the same space. One of them, either her fear or the note, had to go.

The note stayed, and, after a short while, like a snowball rolling down a hill, it grew into a melody. Hannah loved music, but she had never heard anything like this song before. It was as if the music came from someplace where beauty and fun were as common as air.

She peeled her eyes from the hairy, moving mass completely covering her legs and realized the beautiful song was coming from Misty, who was about three steps in front of her. The pod had stopped spinning now that the lower third was submerged. Although Misty sang in a language Hannah didn't recognize, the words magically unscrambled and their meaning became clear. Misty was honoring Hannah and letting her know she was not alone.

Hannah took another step toward Misty. The spidery water now reached the middle of her stomach. The spiders quickly skittered under her shirt and sunk their mandibles into the unprotected skin of her waist and stomach. It felt like a thousand beestings. Hannah screamed and plunged her hands under the water cap, brushing and swatting the spiders from her stomach. As soon as she brushed one layer of spiders away, hundreds more replaced them.

All through Hannah's ordeal, Misty sang her beautiful song of love and encouragement. Hannah gritted her teeth; Misty needed her. She was almost within arm's reach of the pod. Another step or two.

Suddenly, a wave of panic washed over Hannah. Given the slope of the pit, her head would be under the water lid by the time she reached the pod.

The thought terrified her. She was only two small steps from the pod, but now the water was up to her neck and the spiders were biting her back and shoulders. The pain was agonizing. She knew the final steps would submerge her head and give the spiders access to her face, but there was no other way to reach Misty. She remembered Dad's advice for unpleasant situations: "Best to just dive in and get it done right away than to put it off until you feel like doing it or it gets easier because, A—" (Dad always liked to put letters in his advice.) "—chances are you will never feel like doing it, and B, it will never get easier." She would have given anything, anything to see Dad right now.

"Well, here I go, Dad," she whimpered. She took a deep breath, closed her eyes, and plunged forward. Her head slipped under the water cap. The horrible sensation of spiders crawling over her neck and bare face turned her legs to jelly. The spiders fought each other to penetrate her mouth and nose. She slapped the vermin off her face, leaving her stomach undefended. Worst of all, Misty's beautiful song had been replaced by a chorus of *"Snik, snik, snik,"* times ten thousand. It was the sound of thousands of spiders clicking their legs and mandibles as they tried to feast on Hannah's exposed flesh.

She raised one hand, trying to feel the pod containing Misty that, she figured, should be directly over her head. Nothing. She opened her eyes. Bad decision. The spiders lunged for her eyes. Her screams, contained and amplified by the water cap at the top of the pit, only seemed to rev up the spiders as they zeroed in on her stomach, neck, arms, and face. Taking advantage of her scream, a large wood spider skittered into her open mouth.

Hannah gagged and vomited, trying to dislodge the spider. She felt lightheaded, dizzy. Another step, and her legs started to wobble. She was now completely submerged in the spider pool, enveloped from head to toe by a mass of spiders. A wave of nausea surged up her throat. It would not be long, she knew, before the spiders overwhelmed her.

With one last effort, she reached both hands to the surface of the water, no longer making any attempt to fend off the blanket of spiders covering her body.

At first, nothing. Then . . . she felt the pod!

She arched her back and, with a strength she didn't know she had, threw the pod as hard as she could. Whether she had thrown it hard enough for it to clear the edge of the pool, she didn't know. Her dizziness had reached a point that her legs buckled under her weight and the weight of the spiders.

With the last of her strength, she attempted to plunge up the slope and reach the edge of the pool, but her body refused to obey. All she was able to do was raise her spider-bitten face above the water cap for a moment before losing consciousness. In that one brief moment, as the water cap stripped her face of the spiders and she was able to open her eyes without fear, she saw thousands of birds in the trees ringing the pool. Birds—and something else.

On the lower tree branches around the pool perched dozens of beautiful, glimmering fairies. The fairies were armed with bows, swords, spears, and shields and looked really, really angry.

Then darkness overcame Hannah and unconsciousness plunged her into the realm of the pit spiders.

CHAPTER 8

MISTY'S THANKS

Hannah woke to the smell of honeysuckle and wood smoke. When she opened her eyes, spasms of pain shot across her face. It felt like someone had scraped a red-hot fork over every inch of her upper body. Welts covered her torso. Her face was so swollen, it hurt when she winced from the pain. She overheard a discussion near her feet, but it was in a language she couldn't understand. Sleep rescued her from her burning body.

When she woke again, she felt better. Rising to an elbow, she took a look at her surroundings. Panic surged through her when she realized she was still in the spider pool. But there was not a spider in sight. A thick layer of soft green leaves cushioned her from the rocky ground. There was no sign of the water cap that had covered the pool. In its place was a woven reed mat that shielded the enclosure from the sun but somehow let enough light in that she had no trouble seeing most of the enclosure.

"Greetings. Fair weather and a good morning to you, Hannah. It warms my heart to see you have decided to stay." The musical voice came from the shadows at the far side of the pit. "Are you thirsty?"

"Yes," Hannah said, still wary of spiders.

"Do not be concerned about the previous inhabitants of this pool. This place has been cleaned." Misty walked closer, giving Hannah her first clear view of this strange and beautiful creature.

In all, Misty stood no higher than a jar of pickles. Her thick blonde hair was pulled back behind her head and tied with a wisp of sage grass. Her form-fitting short dress appeared to be woven from the petals of meadow flowers, resembling a shimmering rainbow when she moved. She wore no shoes, but around each ankle was tied a silver pendant that flickered when the light caught it just right. On her back was a quiver with arrows no bigger than toothpicks. A small brown pouch the size of a lima bean hung at her waist.

"I am indebted to you, friend," Misty crooned. "Had Brimble not found you when he did, I shudder to think what would have become of my wood."

"What made this place?" Hannah asked, waving her arm around her, which brought a spasm of pain shooting down her side.

"Here, drink this. It will ease the pain and speed the healing." Misty handed Hannah a small cup with no handle, a large pot in relation to Misty's size. Hannah put the cup under her nose and inhaled the sweet aroma of chamomile, cinnamon, and herbal scents.

The tea tasted delicious. As Hannah sipped the steaming liquid, warmth infused her skin, followed by a tingling in her fingers and toes. Because it appeared Misty had forgotten her question as to who or what had created the spider pit, Hannah asked it again.

"It is known as the Feng." Misty's warm and pleasant tone turned harsh. "It is an ancient and dangerous foe. It dug this pit," Misty said, raising an eyebrow, "as a particularly amusing end for someone it particularly despised."

"Who?" Hannah asked. "Who does it despise that much?"

"Why, dear child, that would be me."

CHAPTER 9

MISTY'S MISTAKE

Misty moved closer and settled on a flat rock a few feet in front of Hannah's face. For several minutes, she said nothing, silently staring into the coals of the small fire she had made to heat Hannah's tea. The tingling that Hannah had first felt from the tea was replaced by a relaxing feeling that washed over her body like a warm bath.

"Long ago when I was much younger and the world was already old, life was easier. I had few responsibilities, and I roamed wherever my fancy led me." Misty's eyes never left the fire, and she spoke tentatively, as if the whole of that time could not be told in its entirety but only tasted like a finger dipped in a bowl of frosting.

"As is common among my kind, I had a passion for those things that grow from the earth. Whether it was tree, fern, moss, flower, or weed, if I heard of a particularly interesting or colorful variety, I would travel as far as needed to find it. If it suited me, I would collect a seed, a spore, or a nut so that I would have them when I started my own wood."

"Makes perfect sense," Hannah said, wondering where Misty's story was leading.

"Of all the things that grow, though," Misty continued, standing up to toss a couple of twigs onto the coals, reviving the fire, "I had a special fondness for one beyond all others."

"Which one?" Hanna was curious now.

"Mushrooms. I love the way they look, smell, and taste. Some varieties make excellent soup, some give qualities to medicines that can be found nowhere else, and some are simply fun to look at. I collected spore samples from every mushroom variety I could find and experimented to see which species was best for the climate and soil conditions of my wood.

"One mushroom, however, eluded me. I had heard fragments of stories about it from the elves living near the Harpsreed River. They spoke of a mushroom that looked like a sponge found only at the foot of Froststrife Mountain. The elven name for it is the Spentle. Its taste and fragrance was prized so highly, legend told of a dwarven prince who'd won the heart of the daughter of a sworn enemy by gifting to her a small container of dried Spentle, ending a century-long feud."

"He must have loved her very much," Hannah whispered, picturing the scene clearly.

"The elves seldom ventured to the foot of the mountain to find the Spentle," Misty went on, "because the exotic mushroom was not the only inhabitant of this place. The mountain was guarded by an ancient and intelligent evil known only as the Feng. How long it had lived there, no one knew, for it predated even the oldest records. What was known of the Feng was gathered by the first elves to inhabit Harpsreed River and was delivered to me as a warning when I came looking for the Spentle."

"Excuse me," Hannah asked, shifting positions to take the weight off a particularly sore elbow, "what does this Feng look like?"

"The Feng, in many ways, resembles a giant spider and has command over all spider-kind," Misty said, shifting her gaze for a moment to the edge of the pit and then back to the fire. "It tolerates no one on its land and will pursue any trespassers to the ends of the earth. It can be harmed by blade, arrow, or fire but has a remarkable capacity to heal, making it virtually indestructible. It cannot die."

Hannah shivered, then asked, "Nothing can kill it? Nothing?"

"The elves battled it for a century," Misty answered, "but found no way to cause it any lasting harm. Finally, they formed a protective ring around the forest claimed by the Feng to keep wandering travelers from falling victim to the evil. All this I was told before I entered the land of the Feng in search of my prize. I chose not to heed the warnings."

"Did you find the mushroom?" Hannah asked.

Misty paused for a moment, then, eyes lost in the smoldering embers of the tiny fire, went on.

"My quest ended at the edge of a swift stream bubbling out of the foot of Froststrife Mountain. The Spentle surpassed even the stories I had heard. Small though it was, about so high—" Misty placed her hand about three inches from the ground. "—its fragrance was captivating and could be sensed from a stone's throw away. The smooth base of its stem resembled the trunk of a mighty oak that reached up and held an elongated sponge-like top. The top, with its hundreds of tiny, individual sections, looked as if it had been carved by the hand of a master artisan. I had found my prize.

"I did not have long to enjoy its beauty, though." Misty scooped some pine needles away from the edge of the fire, the pendant around her ankle tinkling softly.

"Please go on," Hannah said quietly, not daring to move lest she break the wood sprite's concentration.

"No sooner had I collected a few spores from the Spentle than the monster was upon me. It had crept up on me while I was admiring the Spentle and attacked me from behind. I slipped out of its grasp and jumped into the raging stream. The current carried me at the speed of a swooping owl, but no matter how fast I was swept downstream, the Feng kept pace on the bank. Finally, with great effort, I was able to swim to safety on the far shore. Exhausted, I turned to see the Feng on the opposite bank jump into the water, still in pursuit of me. The river battered the monster against its stony bottom and swept it out of sight."

"Yea, river!" Hannah cheered, immediately paying for it with a stabbing pain in her cheek.

Misty continued, "My escape was short-lived, for on the morning of the next day, the Feng found me and renewed the chase. It remained that way for several years. I would escape the Feng, and it would find me. I would lay a trap for it, and it would survive. No matter where I went—tree, island, cave—the Feng would follow. It seemed I would live my life in flight, always looking over my shoulder and wondering if the creature was preparing to pounce."

"That must have been horrible," Hannah said, imagining never being able to sleep without fear of being attacked.

Misty stood and took her quiver of arrows from her back, then placed it on the rock at her side. "Finally, I sought refuge in the land of the Druckha, the high elves that guard the giants of the Western Wood beyond the Stormridge Mountains. Because of the entrapments the Druckha used on the border of their land, the Feng met with much pain as it pursued me. It chose to remain outside and wait for me to leave the protection of the Druckha.

"As much as I enjoyed the Druckhas' hospitality, the Feng knew, as did I, I could not stay there forever. Sooner or later, I would leave their protection and the Feng would be waiting. Have no doubt, the Feng is a patient hunter."

"The Feng sounds like a truly horrible creature," Hannah said. "How did you get out of there alive?"

Misty's tone brightened a bit. "One day, as I was pondering my escape, I was visited by Durweil, master craftsman of the Druckha. It was Durweil's devices that had prevented the Feng from following me into the Western Wood. Durweil had studied the Feng and constructed a cage that he thought would contain it if the creature could be captured."

Misty reached into the bean-sized pouch at her side and pulled out a potato. The potato seemed entirely too large to fit in the tiny pouch. Misty set the potato to the side and reached in the pouch again. This time she pulled out a human-sized hairbrush, followed by a roll of yarn, a large strip of birch bark, a leaf bag of birdseed, and a garden trowel. She placed each of these carefully at her side before reaching in for the next item. Finally, she pulled out a small multicolored glass-and-metal box.

The box resembled a large cube, a die with a symbol drawn on each side. Misty pressed her thumb against one side, and the entire side slipped out past the edge of the cube with a click. She did the same with each side. When she had finished, the box appeared as it had before, only now it was twice the size as when she had started. Misty pressed a different side and started the whole process over, once again, ending up with a box twice the size as before.

"How are you doing that?" Hannah squeaked in amazement, watching as the wood sprite "grew" the box by pressing an edge here, sliding a seam there, until the top of the box was over the edge of the pit.

"The Druckha agreed to help me try to capture the Feng. The battle was fierce, and many Druckha were injured by the monster." Misty looked away.

Hannah could see that the memory of the ordeal pained the sprite greatly.

"If not for the unexpected help from one of the three remaining heroes of old, the battle surely would have been lost. Tarvel Rese, a magnificent eastern tiger by appearance, is a champion the likes of which the world has not seen since the Dragon Wars. The battle between the good warrior and the monster lasted three days, but finally, good prevailed and the beast was subdued in this." Misty patted the edge of the box.

"Can this hold the beast?" Hannah stretched to touch the smooth edge of the cube.

Misty moved edges, pushed sides, and slid seams on the wall again. The box began to shrink until it was once again the size of a large die. "Once contained, the terrible evil known as the Feng can be managed quite easily." Misty tucked the cube into her bean purse and fastened the opening by pulling on a string. "It is not gone, but it is contained and can harm no one as long as I keep it within arm's reach of me. While it is here," Misty said, patting the pouch at her waist, "I can sleep without fear of attack. I can go almost anywhere and attend to all the business of the wood. In short, my destiny is once again my own."

"What happens if you don't keep the cube within arm's reach?" Hannah asked.

"Durweil was only able to engineer this incredible device by linking it to my essence."

Hannah scowled. "What's an essence? Is it like a bad smell?"

Misty giggled. "My essence, that unique quality that makes me, me—that thing that no other being in the world possesses, except me—is woven into this device. Unfortunately, a piece of my essence was also captured by the Feng when I trespassed into its land. That is what allows it to find me wherever I am in the world. As a result, if I do not keep the device close, its ability to contain the monster weakens."

Misty stood up and kicked dirt over the dying coals with her bare feet until not even a wisp of smoke remained. "Discussing unpleasant topics, while sometimes necessary, has a way of dimming the world, would you not agree? Let us talk about something more pleasant. What brings you to my wood?"

CHAPTER 10

HANNAH'S CONFESSION

"Dad and I were hiking when I got lost," Hannah said, sitting up and wrapping her arms around her knees.

"If I may be so bold," Misty said, "your father should keep a better eye on you."

"It wasn't his fault! I was distracted and wasn't paying attention to where I was going. Then I was alone except for a bossy old bluebird, Brimble, pulling my hair."

"My wood is beautiful," Misty said with a tone of satisfaction. "Visitors are easily distracted. It has taken many years to achieve what I have done here."

"Yes, your wood is very beautiful," Hannah said quietly. "But that is not what was distracting me."

Misty looked Hannah in the eye and took a step closer. "What bothers you, little one?"

Misty's reference to Hannah as *little* might have amused her under different circumstances, given that Hannah was many times the size of Misty, but the last thing she wanted to do was laugh. For a time, she had forgotten about the life-changing, life-ending news she'd received earlier in the week. Now, it all came rushing back and Hannah bit her lip hard to keep from crying.

Misty stood motionless, arms folded, waiting for Hannah to speak. Hannah stared down at her boots, wishing Misty would not pry into her personal life. Several minutes later, when Misty hadn't batted so much as an eyelash, Hannah concluded that one of the qualities of a wood sprite that Nanna V had failed to mention was *patience*.

Hannah sighed, knowing she might as well confess. "I have diabetes," she whispered.

Misty blinked. "Where is it? If it is in your pocket, I did not see it when I was tending to your wounds."

Hannah could see by Misty's lack of physical reaction—not so much as a frown—that she had never heard of the disease.

"It's a medical condition, and there is no cure." Hannah expected that Misty would act like the kids at school and announce that she had enjoyed their meeting but suddenly remembered she had important people waiting for her to do something far from here.

"Die-bee-tees." Misty enunciated each syllable.

"Yes, that's what I've got." Hannah cringed as if confessing a crime.

"And this die-bee-tees makes you feel sad?" Misty asked.

"Yes, and I will have to live with it for the rest of my life," Hannah said.

"Oh, cattail cotton!" Misty piped, throwing her hands up. "Why did you not say so in the first place? If it is sadness that this thing inflicts on you, we shall take care of that in no time. I will summon Imelda Hollowtree. She always makes me smile with her stories of how, in her youth, she trained chickens to let her ride them and gather berries. I will take you to the waterfall on Blessed Creek where the grassland fairies have bathed for so long that the water has kept bits of their laughter. I shall send a message to the Timmertwill." Misty's eyes lit up, and her breathing quickened. "I will ask him to sing for you a funny song. This die-bee-tees will not have a chance against the songs of the Timmertwill."

"Excuse me," Hannah interrupted. She hated to dampen Misty's enthusiasm but felt the need to clear up a misunderstanding. "Diabetes does more than make you sad."

Misty stopped and looked at Hannah with that unblinking gaze. "Please tell me, what is worse than sad?"

"My body . . . my body has lost its ability to regulate blood sugar levels. If my blood sugar goes too high, I get tired and can end up in the hospital. If it goes too low, I can't think and can end up in the hospital." Hannah glanced at her new friend, trying to read the wood sprite's reaction. What would Misty think of her now?

"Is there any way to keep from getting sick?" Misty asked. "After all, aside from some swelling from your encounter with the pit spiders, you appear to be in good health at the present."

"Yes," said Hannah. "I can keep from getting sick by taking shots and testing my blood sugar several times a day. I also have to watch what I eat and get enough exercise."

"If you do these things, you will stay healthy?" Misty asked.

"Yes, at least I think so. That's what the doctor told me."

"Then, I do not understand," Misty said, honest confusion filling her eyes. "You have this challenge before you, but you have been given ways of overcoming it."

"You don't understand! I can't overcome it! There's no way I can tell you what it's like having diabetes so that you'll understand. It's as if my life is over and I'm worth less than this pit we're sitting in. I'm just not worth anything!"

Hannah sat trembling, eyes squeezed shut, fists clenched. She didn't expect Misty to understand. How could anyone without diabetes understand what she was going through? She waited for Misty to say something, anything, to let her know how she felt about this. Finally, when the silence had gone on so long that Hannah started to wonder if Misty had just picked up and left, she risked a peek.

Misty was still there. She was laughing! Well, not really laughing, but trying her best to conceal a grin that would have looked big on a full-sized person.

CHAPTER 11

IT'S NOT FAIR

"You don't understand. You can't!" Hannah said in a shaky voice.

"I am truly sorry," Misty said, still failing miserably to cover her smile. "It is just that I find that notion amusing."

"What?" Tears filled Hannah's eyes as the anger rose in her throat. "Diabetes is funny?"

Misty's expression grew serious, and she took a step closer and placed her tiny hand on Hannah's knee. "Shaefrond, be at ease; my intention was not to offend."

Hannah turned her head for fear she would start to cry again.

Misty spoke in a gentle but firm tone. "In all creation, only one sort questions their worth: you—your kind, I mean."

Hannah scowled and stared into the darkness of the pit.

"Have you heard of the bog gnomes?" asked Misty.

Hannah refused to look at Misty. Instead, she focused on scratching the innumerable spider bites that encrusted the back of her hands and arms.

Misty folded her arms, and her voice rang with authority like a schoolteacher giving a lecture. "As a whole, bog gnomes contribute next to nothing valuable to the wood. They have no manners and use a disrespectful tone when they speak. They usually sleep until midday, except when my mushrooms ripen, at which time they are up before the sun, raiding my farms. By the time I get there, nothing is left but stems." Misty bent slightly at the waist, her turquoise-green eyes making it clear that her problems with the bog gnomes had a long and serious history.

"Bog gnomes are quite rude and do not even pretend to know the meaning of the expression 'personal hygiene.'" Misty paced back and forth, always staying in Hannah's field of vision, demanding her attention. "They cannot be trusted to do what they say they will do, and if you are foolish enough to lend them something, chances are, you will never see it again. They drink dandelion wine and eat barrels of taffy until late at night, dancing and singing in their off-key, squeaky voices, making it impossible for anyone within a mile of their village to sleep." Misty wasn't finished. "They grow nothing, have no particular talent for anything except drinking, lying, and belching the names of their relatives, and produce nothing except vast quantities of taffy that, on warm days, sticks to everything. They are inconsiderate, boastful, undisciplined, cowardly, and unreliable, and did I mention they have no manners?"

"Yes, I think you might have mentioned that," Hannah said, still trying not to look at the strutting wood sprite.

"My point is just this," Misty said, looking Hannah straight in the eye. "It would be extremely difficult for anyone who meets a bog gnome to conclude exactly how the world is a better place for them having been in it, but if you were to ask the least disciplined and rudest bog gnome if he were 'worth anything,' he would look at you like you had been in the sun too long and then bore you to tears with tales about how incredibly important he is. You humans, on the other hand, are capable of so much more than the bog gnomes." Misty spat the name out as if it put a foul taste in her mouth. "But you spend half of your short lives wondering if you are valuable, worthy, beautiful, or useful. Once you learn you are all of that, and more, you have more years behind you than in front of you, and opportunities have passed. Now, I ask you, does not the notion you are worthless sound a bit absurd?"

Hannah knew she should probably think before answering, but she wasn't ready to give up the point yet. "It's just not fair."

"Why?" asked Misty. "Are you the only one of your kind with this die-bee-tees?"

"No, there are many others," Hannah said, "but it's not fair for them either."

"And these others, they live their lives in sadness and despair?"

"No. Many have done great things," Hannah admitted.

"Can you name one?"

"Nicole Johnson. She's a beauty queen." Hannah had seen the former Miss America speak the year before at a party at Dad's work. It had been an outdoor fair with a band for the grown-ups and pony rides and a clown who made giant balloon fish for the kids. Hannah had to admit, at the time, she had been more interested in the pony rides than in the young woman on the stage, but still, there had been something about her that Hannah liked. True, she was the most beautiful woman, aside from Mom, whom Hannah had seen, but that's not what had made Hannah like her so much. She also seemed really nice, and that was more important. Hannah hadn't known until this week that Nicole was a diabetic even before she was Miss America.

Misty pressed on. "Was this queen of yours treated fairly?"

Hannah did not immediately answer. She needed time to

think, so she picked up leaves from the bed the Fey had made for her and rolled them into shreds between her hands. The crumbs formed a small pile between her boots. After a long pause, Hannah said, "No. I'd heard she had blood sugars so low she almost died and they had to put her in the hospital for several days."

For a moment, nothing more was said. The silence was broken only by the crinkling sound of the leaves in Hannah's hands. Hannah kept her eyes low, ignoring Misty, thinking over their conversation.

Hannah reached for another pile of leaves, but Misty stepped forward and gently pulled a single leaf from Hannah's hand. "You call this plant the violet fern." Misty held the leaf by the stem in front of Hannah's face. "Long ago, a fairy named Feyla Windreed lost her first and only love, Brengae. He gave his life defending her during the war. The battles were fierce and lasted many years. Finally, with the help of a small but courageous group of humans, the dragons and their allies were defeated. But for Feyla, the cost was great. In addition to losing her betrothed in the final battle of the war, she was injured so badly, she was never to fly again." At this, Misty's face clouded over, her mind lost in a place Hannah knew she would never see.

The moment passed, and Misty again focused her attention on the fern leaf held tenderly in her slim fingers. "In tribute to Brengae, Feyla whispered her love for him to this ordinary fern. After a millennium, its leaves looked like this." Misty laid the leaf in Hannah's palm, stem toward her fingertips.

"It's a perfect heart shape," Hannah whispered.

"The fern is a lasting symbol of Feyla's love and her loss, but it was not born of fairness," said Misty. "No, Shaefrond, this fairness you desire is but a shadow. Seek it not, for it will diminish all that you would grow."

CHAPTER 12

SHAEFROND

"Twice now you have called me something," Hannah said. "Is it a name?"
"Shaefrond?"
"Yes," said Hannah. "What does it mean?"
Misty straightened her shoulders and lifted her chin. "It is a name that has been earned by only a handful of your kind. It is in the tongue of the high elves, and it means *friend of the people*, only the *people* it refers to are the Fey. It is a name of power, and it will lift the veil between you and us."
"What veil?" asked Hannah.
"For many ages, the Fey have found it wise to keep hidden from humans. Some, such as the elves and the unicorns, have all but left earth to live in tamer worlds. Those of us remaining have found ways of concealing our presence: shadows, reflections, noisy distractions, to name a few. Have you ever been walking in the wood and thought you saw something

out of the corner of your eye, but when you look right at it, you see only a rock, a bush, or a shadow? That is us."

"So what does a name do about that?" asked Hannah.

"Not just a name," said Misty, "but a title of power bestowed in the old tongue. It will permit you to see many things that previously were hidden from you. Not only will you be able to see us, you will be able to see the things we have made just for our use, such as ladders, bridges, and fountains. You will be entrusted with our history, our secrets, and our wisdom, and you will be welcomed at our festivals and our councils. If you find yourself in danger, you can call on us for assistance. In essence, you will be treated as if you were born to us."

"Why? I mean, what makes me so special?" Hannah couldn't hide her surprise. She couldn't believe what she was hearing. She'd always felt there was something special about this wood but had never imagined it was full of fairy creatures. And now, she'd be able to see them and talk to them! But why her?

Misty raised her eyebrows and let out a tinkling laugh. "Ha. You, my friend, have demonstrated courage of a most remarkable sort. In case you have forgotten, you immersed yourself in a pool of spiders."

Hannah shivered at the memory.

"You did this," Misty continued, "not to save your own life or the life of one you love. Rather, you sacrificed yourself to save the life of a complete stranger. There is goodness in you, *Shaefrond*. And all the folk in my wood will know of it if they do not already. The Timmertwill is already composing a song in your honor."

Hannah caught the same excitement in Misty's voice that she'd heard before when the wood sprite had spoken of the Timmertwill.

"This Timmertwill seems like quite a fellow," Hannah said. "I do hope I will meet him one day."

"Oh, you will, my friend," Misty said, her voice trailing off into a giggle. "He is coming to your party."

"My party! What party?" asked Hannah.

"It has been a full 162 summers since the honor of Shaefrond has been bestowed on one of your kind," Misty said. "True, individual fairies, pixies, or brownies have befriended humans in the past, but that is not the same as being declared a friend to all Fey. It is a great honor, but with it comes great responsibility."

At that moment, a fluttering sound drew Hannah's attention to the top of the pit. Hannah looked up to see a male fairy standing at the edge of the lid. He appeared maybe an inch taller than Misty and was dressed in tanned leather pants and a vest held together in the front by a zig-zag piece of thread. At his waist was a bean pouch similar to Misty's. Like the wood sprite, he had no shoes but wore a forest-green hat that followed the shape of his head. His face had strong features that looked like they had been carved out of oak: high cheekbones, chiseled chin, large blue eyes a few shades darker than Hannah's, and eyebrows that glistened silver, sweeping up at the ends like a bird's wings in flight. He glanced at Hannah and smiled. Leaning forward, he let himself fall into the pit. He gained speed, and just as Hannah started to fear he would fall flat on his face on the rocky ground of the pit, a large pair of blue and orange wings opened from his back. The beautiful wings flapped once, and the fairy gently glided to a stop in front of Hannah and Misty.

"Good day, Guardian," Misty said.

"It is indeed, Meadowatcher. How fares your guest?" The fairy's voice had the same tonal beauty that Misty's had but was much deeper.

"Ask her yourself. Faisle Willowwood—" Misty bent slightly at the waist and waved her arm in Hannah's direction. "—I present to you Shaefrond and my rescuer, Hannah Biel." Misty gestured toward the fairy. "Hannah, I give you Faisle Willowood, master craftsman and present commander of the Fairy Watch."

Faisle tipped his hat in greeting. "It is good to see you did not succumb to the poison of the spiders. How do you fare?"

"Better," Hannah replied, "thanks to this delicious tea. I really would like to learn how you make this."

"And I will enjoy showing you," Misty offered. "The secret is picking the ingredients when the moon is full. We shall have time for this later, but for now, I must attend to a much less pleasant matter."

Misty put her hands on her hips and turned to the fairy at her side. "Faisle, how goes the search?"

Faisle's broad shoulders slumped, and he turned to face the wood sprite. "I bear grim news, Meadowatcher. We found the beast, but not before it attacked an . . . an innocent." Faisle struggled with the last word.

A wave of nausea coursed through Hannah's stomach, creeping up through her chest like the spiders that had recently inflicted her with so much misery. "Tell me about this innocent," Hannah pleaded, fighting her dread at what she might be told.

Faisle glanced at Misty. The wood sprite hesitated, then nodded.

CHAPTER 13

FAISLE'S REPORT

"We had been searching for the beast since we discovered it had escaped."

Misty turned her back to the two and walked into the shadows.

Faisle went on. "We received a report that it had ravaged the village of Verple the bog gnome in Mosquito Flats. When we arrived, we feared the worst. Verple's village was turned upside down. Not a hut was left standing. Bog gnome bodies were scattered throughout the encampment and surrounding trees. When we started collecting the bodies for burial, however, we discovered they were not dead; they were simply dead tired after three straight days of partying. Apparently, the Feng arrived at the camp at the end of Verple's Almost New Moon Festival. Fortunately, not a gnome was coherent enough to put up a fight. The Feng must have considered them unworthy opponents, so he just destroyed their houses and their taffy vats."

"At least they're safe." Hannah knelt close to the fairy.

Faisle continued, "The loss of the homes distressed Verple not at all, but the destruction of the vats was another matter. Verple spit and stomped and waved his arms around his head like he was swatting a swarm of gnats. After raging on for longer than we thought possible, he brought himself under control and swore a blood oath against the Feng. He ordered his people to arm themselves for battle. 'We shall right this wrong,' Verple promised his village, 'if we have to stay up all day to do it.' By the time we left, Verple had decided that vengeance was hard work so it only made sense to visit his cousin's village on Wood Tick Marsh and see if they could spare some buttermilk pastries or rhubarb jelly donuts for the cause."

"You spoke of an innocent," Hannah reminded Faisle.

"We lost the trail of the monster after Verple's village. We were trying to decide what to do when Windglider, the hawk, reported he had seen an unnatural disturbance near the mouth of Purple Turtle Creek. We went there directly and found the place Windglider had described."

"What did you find?" Hannah asked quietly.

"There was no sign of either the Feng or his victim, but it was clear a terrific battle had occurred in the place. Judging by the tracks, a man had been wandering the woods for some time, back and forth, back and forth. He was walking along the creek when the monster attacked him. The man fought bravely, and the battle went up the bank and halfway to the bluff. Finally, the man grew weary and was overcome by the Feng."

Hannah was engrossed in Faisle's story, praying it would have a better ending but fearing the worst. She looked at Misty, who had buried her face in her hands. Hannah drew up her courage and said, "I wish to go to him. Will you take me?"

"We did not find his body," Faisle said, "only bits of his clothing, one shoe, and a case marked with the letter S."

Hannah had hoped that the innocent Faisle had spoken of was not her father, but now her hopes were shattered. Faisle had said the case was marked with an S. This was her diabetic kit that Dad had been carrying. He had marked it with an S for Sunshine, saying when she saw it, she should remember she was like the sun bringing warmth to everyone she touched.

"We tracked the creature to the top of a cliff," Faisle went on, "where it created a massive fortification of webbing at a great tree overhanging the edge. The webbing completely covered the enclosure, leaving not the tiniest opening either on the sides or the top. Despite our best efforts, we were unable to get past the thick, sticky strands that seemed to be made of steel. We suspect the creature is inside, but to what purpose, we know not."

Hannah could contain herself no longer. "No!" she cried. She should have known Dad would never leave the park without her. He must have been sick with worry for her, and now, now he was hurt or worse, and all because of her! Since Mom had left them, Hannah and Dad had been inseparable, a team. They were always there for each other. No matter how hard Dad's day had been at work, he always did or said something to let Hannah know she was important to him. He would tell her how she could brighten the cloudiest day with a smile or sweeten tea with a joke, chase away sickness with a laugh, and melt sadness with a song. When she had been diagnosed with diabetes, Hannah had seen the effect it had on him. It almost seemed as if Dad was more upset than she was, if that was possible.

"No, I won't believe it," Hannah declared firmly. "He can't be dead."

"No, Shaefrond, he is not." Misty spoke from the shadows, the music having left her voice, "but he soon will be."

CHAPTER 14

CALL FOR HELP

"What? How do you know Dad's still alive? What do you know that you're not telling?" A million questions sprang into Hannah's mind.

"For over four hundred summers, the Feng has fasted in the confines of the prison in which I have kept it." Misty appeared from the shadows, her hand touching the pouch at her waist. "Without sustenance, the Feng's once formidable powers have diminished to a fraction of their former strength. All that changes when it feasts on an innocent in the light of a full moon. Once it regains its former strength, it will be unstoppable."

"When is the next full moon?" Hannah was afraid to hear the answer.

"That is why I said your father does not have much time, Shaefrond. The full moon is tonight." Misty looked up at the sky. "In five hours."

"If Dad is in danger, we need to get the police, the fire rescue, the park ranger, the National Guard!" Hannah couldn't bear the thought of Dad all alone at the mercy of a monster. She would get him help, no matter what.

"And tell them what, Hannah?" Misty stepped closer. "That your father has been captured by a giant spider?"

Hannah knew Misty was right. She could picture the reaction from the authorities if she told them her story. "Now there, there, little girl," they would likely say, patting her on the head, "you've had a tough time of it, being lost in the woods for so long. We'll find your dad in the morning." Hannah swallowed hard. She had to keep her head. If she lost control now, she would not be able to think. If she couldn't think, she wouldn't be able to see how to rescue Dad. There must be an answer. All she had to do was think, think, think.

Hannah turned to the wood sprite. "Misty, you were telling me about the benefits of being named Shaefrond, and you said the Shaefrond could call on the Fey for help?"

"Yes, Hannah," Misty said, "in times of dire need, a Shaefrond can request help from the Fey, and they are honor-bound to provide it if they can."

Hannah stood straight, pulled her shoulders back, and, with strength in her voice that surprised her, said, "Then I call on the Fey of your wood to help me free Dad."

Misty and Faisle exchanged wide-eyed glances.

"No, Hannah." It was Faisle this time who addressed the girl. "It is not used in that way. It is for situations when you are lost or attacked by a bear, or need shelter when a sudden storm threatens your safety. It has never been used to enlist all Fey-kind to rescue a human who is unknown to them."

"He's not just a *human*," Hannah shouted, turning to Faisle with her fists on her hips. "He's my dad! We have to do something."

"We have no chance, Hannah," Misty said. "Even in its weakened state, the Feng will overcome you and me with little effort. Besides, you are not yet fit to travel."

Hannah wanted to lash out and tell them how wrong they were. She felt fine. But then she looked down at her spider-bitten arms oozing a clear fluid. Her whole body itched, and she could smell a putrid odor as the spiders' venom oozed out of her body. She wanted nothing more than to take a bath and put the spider pit behind her. Maybe Misty was right. How could she help Dad in her condition? She remembered what Misty had said about the Feng: It was an ancient and intelligent monster. She'd seen what it had done to the clearing around the pool. Small trees had been completely uprooted. What could she possibly do in her condition against such power?

The wisp of a song flitted through her mind, the song Dad sang every morning when he woke her. It was a song about Noah and the ark: "Rise and shine and give God the glory, glory." it began. By the time the song got to what Noah put on the ark, she would be giggling because Dad could never remember the names of the animals. That didn't slow him at all, though, because he would make up his own animals to rhyme with the previous line in the song. On Dad's ark, there were "chimpookers" and "dogadookies" and "ratimbalos." Hannah could never fall back to sleep after trying to figure out what a "ratimbalo" looked like.

Hannah gritted her teeth, sending a jolt of pain along her jawline and down the side of her neck. "If you won't help me save him, I ask you to kindly show me where he is so I can do it myself."

Faisle and Misty gasped. Finally, Misty made a bow toward Hannah and said, "Please excuse me." Misty walked up the slope of the pit and disappeared over the edge. Without a word, Faisle tipped his hat to Hannah, took a couple of quick steps, and, with a flurry of his colorful wings, went skittering up and over the roof of the enclosure. Hannah found herself alone in the bottom of the pit.

CHAPTER 15

ALONE AGAIN

Misty's and Faisle's abrupt departure left Hannah wondering what she was going to do. How could she find Dad without help? She doubted she would even be able to make it out of the woods without directions. Despite the night she had spent under Misty's care and the wood sprite's wonderful tea, she looked, felt, and smelled dirtier than she had ever been before in her life. Every inch of her body itched. Then a thought crept into her mind like a spider preparing to pounce on a fly.

She had no idea of her blood sugar level. She hadn't eaten for a day and a half, and her body had gone through all kinds of trauma battling the spiders. She could not tell whether the nausea she was feeling was a result of the spider venom or her blood sugar being too high or too low. If only she had the kit Dad had carried with him when they had started hiking, she would be able to test her blood sugar and adjust her level. The thought of having a low-blood-sugar spell all alone in the woods terrified her almost as much as the spider pit had.

Hannah sat for a while in the silence and emptiness of the pit, considering her options. Faisle had described the monster's lair as a high place at the top of a cliff. She wondered if he was referring to the lookout at the top of Bigley Bluff where one could see miles of the great river and the grassy green plains of South Dakota. The view was awesome but a bit scary because of the sheer drop-off at the edge of the lookout. She had trouble imagining Dad being held captive by a fiend in that beautiful place, but that was the only one she could think of that matched Faisle's description.

Hannah's thoughts were interrupted by a commotion outside the pit. It sounded like an argument. She decided there was nothing to be gained by staying where she was, so she slowly started to climb up the slope and out of the pit.

After the events of the past day and a half, Hannah figured she was beyond being surprised by anything. After all, she'd seen several curious things. She'd seen a pit full of spiders that were kept in place by a water lid that didn't obey the laws of gravity. She'd seen and talked to a well-mannered wood sprite that could have fit into the thermos she used for school. And she'd met a handsome fairy with blue and orange wings.

Already, she knew if she ever got out to tell this story, there was no one, outside of maybe Nanna V, who would believe her.

As Hannah reached the top edge of the pit, a bustling circus of light, sound, and color filled her eyes. At the edge of the clearing twinkled dozens of small fairy-like creatures, some she recognized as gnomes—two of whom were arguing over which had drunk the last sip of nectar—with their stocky build and pointy hats. Among the gnomes were slim pixies with their narrow wings, short hair, and colorful, form-fitting shirts, and also brownies, who looked like miniature old men and women, each carrying a cane or a staff. Others were totally outrageous, like the oversized orange butterfly with shiny white boots and the two-foot long, purple snail with full red lips and eyelashes. These were some unusual creatures that not even Nanna V had mentioned before.

Streaking blurs of brown, green, and blue flashed through the clearing. The blurs would stop at various points along the clearing and then, *zip!* they'd be off again before Hannah could really make them out. Hannah remembered a trick Dad had taught her for seeing stuff that was moving really fast, like ceiling fans or her cat, Tiny, when he was chasing a mouse. All she had to do was close her eyes at the right time, and she could see a snapshot of what was happening. After a couple of misses, she got it just right.

The blurs were fairies. Not fairies like Faisle, but smaller and much faster. They were only about three inches long and moved with lightning speed. Their outfits of brown, green, or blue explained why they looked like streaks of color when they were moving, which was most of the time. Each place they stopped, they picked up a twig, straightened a bent piece of grass, or mended a torn leaf. Hannah assumed the miniature brown fairies attending to the broken trees and bushes were forest fairies. She figured the green fairies mending the grasses were grassland fairies and the blue fairies that stopped wherever the other fairies had been and sprinkled a shiny blue dust that left the grass, leaf, or tree with a wet sheen must be water fairies. Hannah smiled as she came to understand that these fairies were healing the clearing and fixing the damage done by the Feng.

"Are you having problems with your eyes?" the snail, who introduced herself as Priscilla, slowly asked.

Still trying to figure out what this was all about, Hannah did not immediately respond.

"I might have something in my purse to help your condition. Pardon me. I won't be long." Priscilla batted her giant eyelashes once and turned her large purple shell, or rather, started to turn very slowly toward the edge of the clearing.

CHAPTER 16

THE FEY HOST

"Have you met everyone?" Misty walked to the edge of the pit, and a hush fell over the assembled Fey.

"No, I haven't," Hannah said, running her fingers through her hair. She was suddenly very aware of how awful she must look. Her hair was matted to the side of her head. The spider bites that covered her entire upper body were still oozing slightly and had left her skin caked with a crusty, scabby film that smelled like rotten eggs. Her blue T-shirt and jeans were filthy and looked like they would never be clean enough to wear again.

"How are you feeling?" Misty asked.

"Pretty good," said Hannah, trying to pull some hair that was stuck to the side of her face away from her eyes. Her skin itched everywhere she could reach and a few places she couldn't, but the swelling was gone, and it didn't hurt every time she moved.

"If you would permit, I know someone who might be able to help you feel more like yourself," Misty said.

Hannah just nodded as she finger-combed her hair.

Misty turned to the forest and said a word that sounded like the wind. *Whooshta.* A deep-blue water fairy zipped from the edge of the clearing and stopped in front of Misty. The two had a brief conversation that Hannah couldn't hear. Now and then, the fairy looked over Misty's shoulder at Hannah and smiled, nodding her head and giggling once. Then, *zip!*, she was gone. Misty turned back to Hannah and smiled. Hannah waited for Misty to speak, but the wood sprite just kept looking at Hannah, smiling.

Suddenly, Whooshta streaked over the edge of the pit straight at Hannah's face. Hannah tried to duck, but the moment before the fairy should have collided with the end of Hannah's nose, she changed directions and ended up just above the girl's head. The fairy was followed by another, and another, and another, until a dozen blue fairies hovered in a small circle over Hannah's head. Hannah felt something wet run down the back of her neck. Soon, her entire head was soaked and big drops of blue water dripped off her forehead onto the ground. The volume of water increased until Hannah was covered in a steady shower of blue water soaking her entire body, hair, and clothing.

The water was warm and felt wonderful as it washed the smelly spider ooze from her body and clothes. Finally, the gush stopped and Hannah wiped her eyes.

"Thank—" She didn't get to finish. A wave of forest and grassland fairies rushed her from the edge of the clearing. The forest fairies zipped a spiral pattern around her body, starting at her boots and ending at her head. Soon, Hannah smelled an aroma between cinnamon and baking soda and noticed foam bubbling all over her. She blew suds from her face only to see it collide with a spiraling fairy. The fairy dropped out of the spiral, spun twice, and landed with a thud at Hannah's feet.

"Sorry," Hannah apologized, "are you OK?"

"No harm done." The fairy winked, wiped her face with a sleeve, and zipped back into the spiral before Hannah could say more.

Now the fairies started to scrub her with their pine needle brushes. The sensation of being scrubbed all over by a dozen speeding fairies tickled Hannah, and soon she was giggling and wiggling her arms.

Next, the water fairies returned and poured water over Hannah, rinsing her suds, dirt, and scum to the bottom of the pit. The grassland fairies came next, detangling her hair while the others spun around her body so fast they created a warm breeze that, in a few minutes, dried her clothing and skin. The fairies working on her hair did not take part in this but remained focused on their task. One would pull a strand straight out from her head, and another would run a tiny comb from her scalp to the end of the strand. Within no time, all the knots and tangles were gone, and Hannah was feeling better than she had in a long time. But the fairies weren't done.

After they straightened her hair, about a third of the fairies started working on it, pulling, twisting, and combing, while the rest zipped back and forth into the woods. There was so much buzzing activity around Hannah's head, she had trouble seeing how the fairies coming and going from the wood did so without crashing into each other.

Finally, the fairies stopped pulling, twisting, and combing her hair and hovered a foot in front of her face like a dozen hummingbirds. Each pulled from its pocket a tiny mirror, and they held the mirrors together to form one large mirror. Hannah's mouth dropped open when she saw her transformation.

Like the water fairies in front of her, the forest and grassland fairies had formed large mirrors behind Hannah, giving her a complete view of the back of her head.

The strands of her hair had been individually tied into little bundles of about ten strands each. At various points along each bundle, tiny blossoms of blue, green, and orange had been woven to form a colorful three-dimensional picture of a magnificent orange tiger sharpening his claws on a tree. As Hannah moved her head, the hair shifted and the picture came alive. The tiger twitched his tail, turned his head, and opened his jaws as if to growl. Hannah stood speechless. It was enchanting, and she felt more beautiful than she had in a long time.

Hannah's trance was broken by Priscilla, who had not moved a foot from where Hannah had first seen her.

"Is there something wrong with your mouth?" Priscilla drawled. "I might have something in my purse to help that as well." Priscilla batted her eyelashes once and, ever so slowly, turned toward the forest.

"You like?" asked Whooshta.

Hannah lightly touched a bundle of hair on the side of her head, careful not to disturb any of the blossoms woven into it so skillfully by the fairies. "Yes, very much," she murmured, admiring her reflection in the fairy mirrors. "Thank you!"

Misty walked to the edge of the pit and beckoned Hannah to stand beside her so all the Fey could see her. Hannah stepped away from the soggy ground caused by her cleansing and stood next to Misty. The assembled Fey—stood quietly around the clearing, watching her, waiting for her to speak.

"Friends and fellow guardians of the wood." Misty's voice was gentle but carried over the clearing with the firmness of authority. "I thank you for answering my call and the call of Hannah, Shaefrond, and friend of all Fey. Each of you came of your own free will and is under no obligation to stay, though

I urge you to hear Hannah's plea and heed her call for help. Her need is great, and the danger she faces is not from her world but from ours." Misty touched her pouch.

All eyes turned to Hannah, and a heavy silence filled the clearing.

Misty reached into her bean pouch and, like before, pulled several objects from it that seemed entirely too large to fit in the tiny space of the pouch: a sea shell, a reference book on herbs, a can opener, and a wooden spoon. Finally, she pulled out a black case marked with a large silver S and handed it to Hannah.

"The Fey are assembled, my friend," Misty said with a slight bow of her head, "and are eager to hear how you would rescue your father."

CHAPTER 17

FIRST THINGS FIRST

Hannah thanked Misty and wasted no time. Quickly, she opened the kit to find it just as she and Dad had packed it: alcohol swabs for cleaning her skin, meter and test strips for measuring her blood sugar levels, several packets of sugar tablets in case her blood sugar went low, two small bottles of insulin, and several syringes.

Hannah ripped open an alcohol pad and wiped her finger. As she did so, she noticed the Fey watching her from around the clearing.

That's OK, she thought, *this is important, and if I'm going to help Dad, I'm going to have to be at my best.* Her blood level turned out to be a little high and required only a slight adjustment of insulin. Hannah wiped the bottles of insulin—she had both the fast-acting and the long-acting kinds in her kit—with an alcohol swab and removed a syringe from the case. She carefully inserted the end of the syringe into the bottle and pulled the plunger back to fill the syringe with the proper amount of insulin, lifted the bottom of her shirt, and, using the same alcohol swab she'd used to clean the bottle, wiped a small spot on her stomach. Remembering Dad's advice about not waiting to do unpleasant things, she snapped her wrist and plunged the half-inch needle into her belly. She barely felt the needle. "Thank you, Dad," she whispered, remembering how he'd insisted on getting her the thinnest possible needles. After she pushed the insulin into her belly, she pulled the needle out and, again, cleaned her skin with the swab. She put everything away and looked up to see the entire host of Fey still watching her.

Well, they haven't run away, she thought. *I guess I should be happy about that.* But what would they think of her now? Would they still be willing to help her rescue Dad? She didn't have to wait long for an answer.

"Do you like peaches?" asked Priscilla, who had not moved an inch from where Hannah had last seen her.

Hannah smiled as she told Priscilla that peaches were one of her favorite foods.

Like Priscilla, the rest of the Fey seemed not mind that Hannah was diabetic. Except for Priscilla who went on about the peach cobbler recipe she'd inherited from her grandmother and her promise to make it for Hannah's party, the Fey waited patiently for Hannah to tell them how she planned to rescue her father.

CHAPTER 18

MICHAEL'S CAGE

Hannah's dad assessed his situation, and it did not look good. Michael had faced many horrible things in his life—his wife's death and Hannah's diabetes diagnosis, for example—but this was out of a nightmare. He judged the strength of the branch that held him upside down suspended 200 feet above the Missouri River. The branch seemed strong enough to bear his weight, but each time he struggled trying to free himself, the branch bent to near breaking point. The branch was attached to a tree completely encircled with webbing, leaving him no escape other than through the monster.

Not six feet away, with legs sprawled among the branches of the tree, sat the monster. The creature resembled a giant tarantula, with short dark hair covering its legs and oversized stomach, but this fiend, apart from its enormous size, had some differences that made it unlike any spider Michael had ever seen. First, its legs were not skinny like a normal spider's but were rather thick and segmented with muscle that seemed to roll under the skin whenever the creature moved. Second, each leg ended not in a point, like those of other spiders, but in a small hand that gripped branches and prey with enormous strength, as Michael had learned in their battle by the creek. Third, the mouth did not consist of mandibles that pinched inward but of long white fangs that curved downward like the tusks of a walrus.

Then there were the monster's eyes. Its eyes bore no resemblance to the round, unintelligent eyes of an insect. The two oversized eyes were tapered at the ends like human eyes but reflected a deep hatred of all that was good or beautiful. These were the eyes of evil, and they sent a cold shiver across Michael's shoulders whenever the creature looked at him. Luckily, the fiend mostly kept its eyes fixed in the direction of the edge of the clearing and the setting sun.

Michael decided there was no point trying to make sense of what had had happened. If the panic he'd felt when he realized he'd lost Hannah wasn't enough, being attacked by a giant spider-monster took the prize. What was it, and where did it come from? Why was it keeping him? And worst of all, did it have something to do with Hannah's disappearance?

The webbing wrapped around his body kept Michael's hands firmly ensnared and flat against his sides. With great effort, he was able to move the fingers of one hand just enough to loosen the strands lashing his hand to his side. If he could free that hand, he might be able to reach the pocketknife on his belt. He wrenched his right shoulder hard, straining until the muscle was on fire. His fingertips touched the knife. He grasped it, flicked it open, and quietly sawed at the strands around his waist.

What was he going to do when he freed himself? Even if he were somehow able to escape the webbing, he would have to climb up the branch suspending him, if it held, and fight the monster while standing in a tree overhanging a cliff. By the looks of the shadows, it would be dark soon.

Well, as he always told Hannah, there was nothing to be gained by putting off unpleasant tasks. Michael grabbed the branch with his now free left hand. One more slice of the knife, and his legs would be free and he would be on his way to finding Hannah. He was absolutely committed to do it—or to die trying. He couldn't stand to think of his Sunshine spending another night alone in these woods with this predator on the loose.

As Michael was quietly sawing through the webbing around his ankles, he heard a *thump*, followed by a *click*, followed again by a *thump*. The sound, which was coming from the woods, picked up pace: *thump, click, thump, click, thump, click,* and, every once in a while, *pppprmp*.

The giant spider peered in the direction of the sound, moving its head from side to side, trying to see through the strands of its own webbing. Michael decided to wait a moment before making the final cut that would free his legs.

CHAPTER 19

SETTING THE TRAP

Hannah stood at the edge of the wood, her eyes never leaving the webbing that imprisoned her father. Just as she had hoped, the sound of Misty unfolding the cage was disguised by the sound of the Fey instruments. When the cage was at its full size, the forest and grassland fairies had little trouble camouflaging it with twigs, branches, and weeds to make it blend in with the rest of the forest floor at the top of the bluff. The cage had been placed, open side up, in a hollow depression under a fallen ash tree. Verple and several of his bog gnomes had actually been helpful in digging out the depression and making it deeper so the cage could fit.

Now, she thought, *all we have to do is get the Feng to come out and stand on top of the cage opening.* The twigs placed over the cage should then give way, dropping the monster into the cage. Misty would be standing by ready to close the lid. It was a dangerous plan with little room for error, but Hannah could think of no other way to save Dad in the little time they had before dark and the full moon.

A quick look around the clearing showed that all were ready. Hannah gave Misty a nod and braced herself for what was to come.

Misty walked behind the line of Fey, offering encouragement with a word, a smile, or a gentle touch on the shoulder. Hannah understood the purpose of the act as the small warriors released held breaths, loosened white-knuckled grips on weapons, or, in a few cases, returned Misty's smile.

Misty stopped behind a tall fellow with wild hair who looked to be neither fairy, sprite, nor gnome. He wore a long coat decorated with multicolored patches sewn into the fabric, each patch embroidered with a bird, a leaf, a fish, or some animal that Hannah didn't recognize. A wide blue headband did little to contain waves of thick, coal-black hair that darted in every direction as if trying to escape the fellow's head before coming to rest across his broad shoulders. His face did not have the windswept features of the Fey, with their high cheekbones and tilting eyes, but bore an aura of cheer as if smiling came to it as easily as breathing.

Misty stood on her tiptoes to put her chin above the fellow's shoulder, whispered something into his ear, then turned on her heel and walked back down the line of Fey toward Hannah. The fellow stood motionless, mouth hanging open, wide eyes following Misty's retreating form. Before Misty reached Hannah, the fellow stooped and pulled a pine nut from a cone half buried in the forest floor at his feet. He cupped his hands around the nut, placed it up to his mouth, and spoke a word. With a flick of his wrist, he hurled the nut so it traveled in an arc over the Fey in Misty's direction, appearing to Hannah as if the nut would land in Misty's hair.

When the nut was above Misty's head, however, it *popped*, blowing out a shower of white rose petals that cascaded over Misty as she walked the last few steps to stand beside Hannah.

The Timmertwill? Hannah could see by Misty's beaming smile that reached even the wood sprite's eyes, she didn't need to ask.

The Timmertwill pulled an instrument from his coat and began to play.

* * *

When the music started, it appeared to Michael as if the monster was being slowly roasted over a fire. The short hairs on its back bristled. The muscles of its legs shuddered. Its white-knuckled hands gripped the branches of the enclosure. Michael couldn't figure out what was enraging the creature so much.

The music, gently riding on top of the rhythmic beat, was no less than a beautiful symphony. Michael was unable to identify the instrument being played. It sounded close to a flute or clarinet, but the tones were more pleasant and calming than any he'd heard before. The music grew until he could hear lutes and pipes and bells and strings being blown and struck and plucked all in perfect harmony, timing, and pitch as if he'd woken in a great concert hall and was being entertained by world-class musicians.

The very peacefulness of the music that comforted and enchanted Michael had the opposite effect on the monster. The spider's legs froze in place. Slowly, the monster lowered its head and closed its dark eyes.

Michael didn't know what the monster was planning but knew it couldn't be good.

CHAPTER 20

AMBUSH

Faisle was the first to see the horde of spiders rushing the rescuers from behind. "Look to the rear!" All the Fey who had gathered around the clearing preparing to battle the Feng had been focused on the web-covered tree at the edge of the cliff rather than on the forest behind them.

Hannah turned and almost collapsed in fear. Wave after wave of spiders covered the forest floor and the trunks of the trees, with seemingly thousands of the hairy little beasts charging the small group at the top of the bluff. Hannah whirled around, looking for some way to escape—and stopped short as she realized what the spiders were doing. The spider army was driving her band of rescuers toward the edge of the cliff.

Faisle quickly formed the Fairy Guard into a ground line that would intercept the charging spiders. Each fairy was armed with a sword or staff and had a small bow strapped to his or her back. Hannah could not understand how the fairies could stand motionless, waiting for the mass of spiders, many of which measured waist-high to them.

Within seconds of Faisle positioning his guards, the first of the spiders were upon them. Faisle's small group of warriors fought bravely and completely stopped the first wave of spiders. The second wave was stronger than the first and drove the guards into the lower branches of the trees, where the guards and the pixies drew their bows and fired arrow after arrow at the charging horde.

On the ground, the Fey who could not fly were slowly being forced to the edge of the cliff.

"Stop!" Hannah cried, desperately trying to stuff her pants legs under her socks. "Fight them where you stand, or we'll all be swimming in the Muddy Mo'!" Hannah gestured to the Missouri River, which awaited them at the bottom of the cliff.

The Fey stopped their retreat, realizing the wisdom of Hannah's words. Quickly forming themselves into small defensive groups, the Fey fought the spiders back to back. Misty climbed atop Priscilla's shell, the snail moving with surprising speed, and put herself between Hannah and the bulk of the spider army.

When the spider wave attacked Misty, Priscilla's large pink tongue darted out and swabbed up all spiders within her reach. Gob after gob of spiders swept past Priscilla's bright red lips and into her gaping mouth. Any spiders that made it past her whipping tongue met a flashing golden sword wielded by Misty, who, still perched on Priscilla's back, thrust and parried with incredible speed.

The rescuers fought bravely, but Hannah quickly realized that the sheer number of the spiders would overwhelm them before long. There were just too many. The fairies and pixies, having run out of arrows, flew overhead, dropping sticks and rocks on the spiders. Verple and his small band of bog gnomes were nowhere to be seen. Despite Hannah's warning, the ground Fey now stood only feet away from the sheer drop of the cliff.

Just when Hannah thought all was lost, Misty sprang from Priscilla's back and shouted, "Imelda! You could not possibly be more tardy!"

Hannah looked down the slope and saw a rather large, old brownie perched on a rather large, blue-headed chicken racing directly toward them. "Sorry I am late," giggled the rider. "I had to ask some friends for help. I hope I didn't miss much."

Hannah guessed the large chicken rider was none other than the legendary Imelda Hollowtree, and Hannah knew well the blue-headed chicken she was riding. It was Gordon, Nanna V's pet rooster. She soon saw the friends Imelda was talking about as a dozen more of Nanna V's chickens raced up behind the brownie and Gordon.

Imelda and the chickens cut straight through the mass of spiders like a lawnmower through spring grass. The chickens plucked and pecked at the spiders with speed and accuracy, as if they'd been doing it all their lives—which, in truth, they had. They were soon joined by a host of starlings, blue jays, cardinals, chickadees, and one red-tailed hawk led by Brimble.

The spiders skittered back down the hill or over the cliff in their mad attempt to escape their natural enemy. Imelda and her chickens pursued the spiders down the hill until neither chicken nor spider could be seen.

Hannah watched the Fey collect their arrows and return to their places around the clearing. She wondered if they would have the courage to stick to her plan for rescuing Dad.

She didn't have to wonder for long. The Timmertwill began to play a slow, sad melody with his unique instrument that resembled two green clarinets tied side by side. The song started softly, then rose in volume and tempo until it filled the wood with its pure goodness. The warm and gentle tones seemed to calm the rescuers. Although she hadn't heard the song since she was a little girl, Hannah knew it well, remembering how her mom would sing it while bathing her or braiding her hair. Without thinking, and without really intending to, Hannah found herself singing along with the music.

* * *

Michael froze. The sound of Hannah's beautiful voice filled him with both joy and panic. What was she doing here? He was thrilled to realize she was alive and, judging by the strength of her clear voice, uninjured, but the thought of her near the monster was more than he could bear.

More disturbing to Michael than the thought of Hannah being near this monster was the reaction that his captor was having to Hannah's voice. It was as if the creature had been stabbed in the stomach with a flaming sword. It was clear to Michael that the beast wanted nothing more than to stop the sound that was inflicting so much pain.

At the moment Michael realized the beast intended to harm Hannah, his plan was set. One more slash of his knife, and his legs would be free. With a little effort, he should be able to pounce on the creature's back and pull it over the cliff into the river below. He knew it would probably mean the end of him, but there was no way he was going to let this monster harm his daughter.

Michael quickly freed his feet from the webbing and with one movement swung his legs below him and hoisted himself to the branch above his head. This position would give him a good vantage point from which to jump on the beast. The monster seemed totally unaware of what was happening behind it. It was still transfixed by Hannah's voice. Michael crouched and, with his puny knife held high, leaped.

The very moment Michael leaped, the creature let out a terrifying groan. *RRAAARrrrsk!* In one massive movement, the creature's eight hands shattered the webbing and it charged onto the bluff.

Michael fell into empty space.

CHAPTER 21

VERPLE'S CONTRIBUTION

Even though everything—almost everything—was going according to plan, the rescuers were not ready for the speed and ferocity of the Feng. It moved so quickly with its eight powerful legs that it pounced upon them before any could react.

Hannah had felt she had a good idea of what the Feng looked like based on Misty's descriptions, but she was still shocked at the monster's pure ugliness. Like an enraged bull with black hair bristling and froth dripping from its fangs, the monster threw up a dust cloud as it charged straight at her.

Hannah had placed herself behind the cage so the creature would have to cross the trap to get to her. The plan seemed to be working as the Feng made a beeline directly for her. The monster came closer, and Hannah held her ground, not moving an inch. If she lost her courage and ran, the Feng might change directions and miss the trap. Three steps, two, one step farther, and it would be snared. Misty stayed hidden, ready to close the lid.

Suddenly, the Feng froze. It stared at the ground in front of it. The Fey exchanged wary glances. What was going on?

"What's the matter, creepy monster," Hannah questioned in her best Dora Sheckler imitation, "do I frighten you?"

Aaaarrrrw! The monster's shriek reminded Hannah of a snake made of thunder and smoke. The Feng crouched, preparing to pounce, but just before it stepped on the trap, Verple appeared on a branch thirty feet above their heads. A couple of his fellow bog gnomes stuck their heads out of an abandoned bees' nest a few feet away from him. Apparently considering himself safely out of reach, Verple began to tell the "beetle scum" what he was going to do to it for destroying his taffy vats.

"Stop, you fool!" hissed Hannah, but Verple took no notice and continued to insult the Feng in language only a bog gnome could fully appreciate.

"What is that smell?" Verple asked with a crinkled nose. "Oh, it's you," he said, gesturing to the Feng. "I've got a suggestion for you, mister. The next time you bathe, you should do it in water instead of sour cheese and skunk snot."

This insult brought loud hoots of laughter from the gnomes still in the bees' nest. The monster was not amused. With the quickness of a horse kick, the fiend lashed out an arm and struck a mighty blow to the trunk of Verple's tree so forcefully that it sent chunks of bark flying and shook the ground beneath Hannah's feet. The blow also dislodged Verple from the safety of his limb and sent him plummeting down through the leaves. Verple stopped with a hollow *thump!* on the lid of the trap. The lid held for a moment, then, with a loud *snap!* gave way, taking most of the covering and a wide-eyed Verple with it to the bottom of the cage.

"HARRRSK! *Now you will dieeeeee.*" The monster's voice grated like a metal barrel being dragged across gravel.

Seeing that their trap had failed, the Fey sprang into action. Faisle's Guard were the first to move. They dove in, launching rocks and spears at the Feng. The grassland, forest, and water fairies attacked, wrapping grass, weeds, and vines around the beast's legs. To Hannah, it seemed as though the monster was wearing rainbow stockings. Misty drew her bow and fired a dozen arrows in as many seconds into the monster's head. Hannah watched with surprise as each wound inflicted on the monster healed almost immediately, the arrows springing out of the creature like popcorn.

With a mighty burst, the Feng snapped the vines on its legs and reared on its hind legs. The Feng shot a thick stream of webbing towards the Fey like a fire hose uncoiling and springing from its stomach, covering them with brown, syrupy goo. The attacking fairies dropped to the ground like ripe acorns. The Feng pounced on them in seconds and rolled them into one giant ball of webbing.

"Run, Shaefrond!" Misty urged quietly.

Hannah bolted, but not in the direction Misty had pointed. Rather than turning back and scooting down the bluff away from the monster, she hurried toward the cliff and the web-covered tree where she believed the monster had imprisoned Dad. She had to go at an angle to avoid the Feng directly in her path.

She was halfway to the tree when the Feng turned toward her. The Feng blocked her path, placing itself with its back to the cliff. The corners of its misshapen hairy mouth, with its two protruding oversized fangs, turned up in what seemed a hideous smile. Hannah tried to run but was held in place by the Feng's evil gaze. Her feet seemed stuck in the ground as if she were a tree rooted deep in the rocky bluff. The Feng was so close, its decaying stench nearly made her vomit.

Suddenly, the flash of a golden sword and blonde hair passed between Hannah and the Feng. Misty moved with the agility of a squirrel and the speed of a jackrabbit. Armed with her sword of gold, she was all over the Feng, slashing, thrusting, poking, and ripping. The monster desperately tried to fend off Misty's attack, pounding at her with its eight hands, but Misty was always a bit too fast, darting away before the creature's blows could land. Many times the creature's strikes missed Misty and dented its own coarse, hairy hide.

Hannah could see how the Feng was tiring, slowing because of the damage Misty, the brave little warrior, was inflicting on it. Misty's blows rained down faster than the monster could regenerate.

Suddenly, the Feng stopped trying to swat Misty and began to spin in tight circles while spraying a sticky version of the webbing onto itself.

"Watch out!" Hannah called when she realized what the Feng was doing. Her warning came too late.

Misty's golden sword became stuck in the gooey mess. When she put her foot against the Feng to pull the sword free, her foot became stuck also. The Feng had turned itself into a giant glue trap.

Before Hannah could react, the Feng turned and flung a wad of the sticky substance at her feet. She tried to move, but her boots seemed nailed to the ground.

The Feng jerked Misty from its body and fastened her with webbing to a nearby tree so that all that could be seen of her was her head and toes. *"You, I will sssave for lassssst!"* the monster spat at the wood sprite.

While the Feng was preoccupied with Misty, Hannah looked around for some weapon she could use against it, for she knew it would come for her next. She saw nothing in her reach but a few broken branches and some small rocks. She had nothing on her body except what she was wearing and her diabetes kit fastened to her belt.

Rescuing Dad was going nothing like she had planned. She was too close to give up now, but what could she do? She had nothing resembling a weapon, and the monster had stopped all of her friends, just as Misty had predicted.

Hannah cringed when the Feng turned its dripping maw toward her. She wanted nothing more than to bolt from this hideous fiend, but her feet were firmly fastened to the ground by the goo that was quickly hardening into fibrous strands.

Seeing that Hannah was going nowhere, the creature turned around and placed its massive hairy back to her and the setting sun.

"There isssss time," the Feng said. It began to clean itself of the sticky mess.

CHAPTER 22

TRAPPED

Hannah's mind reeled as she sought a solution. With all her strength, she tried to pry loose her legs, but they wouldn't budge, and she almost fell over in the process. Think, she must think. There must be an answer.

Her hands began to shake. She quickly felt her forehead and found it was wet with cold sweat. The nausea that she hadn't noticed until now confirmed her fear. Her blood sugar had dropped, and she was going into hypoglycemia. Hannah knew from her previous episodes of low blood sugar that if she didn't eat something sweet soon, her thinking would slow.

No! Hannah screamed silently. *I must be able to think, or all is lost.* With trembling hands, she reached for her diabetes kit at her waist. She quickly unzipped the kit and popped a couple of sugar tablets in her mouth. As she chewed the tablets, an idea came to her. It was a wild plan—Dora Sheckler would say it was stupid—and she knew what the creature would do to her if it caught her, but she saw no other way.

It didn't take long for her to find a spot that would work. Inches in front of her was a bare spot on the monster's back with a bulging vein. This would be perfect. With a bit of luck, the creature wouldn't even feel the tiny needle pierce its tough hide.

Quickly, she pulled a syringe and a bottle of the fast-acting insulin out of her kit.

On her first attempt to get the needle in the bottle, her hands were shaking so badly that she missed the bottle and stuck the needle in her finger.

"Ahh—" Hannah snapped her mouth shut. The monster stiffened. Hannah froze. The Feng started to turn its head, but something drew its attention in the direction of the webbed tree at the edge of the bluff.

Hannah knew this was her one and only chance. She steadied the hand holding the bottle on her leg and made another attempt to stick the needle into the tiny rubber circle at the top of the bottle.

Yes! The needle sank into the bottle. She quickly depressed the plunger, turned the bottle upside down, then pulled the plunger back as fast as it would let her, filling the entire syringe with fast-acting insulin—many times the amount she would use for herself. A glance over the creature's back showed it was still intently watching the edge of the cliff twenty feet away.

Hannah raised the syringe in her shaking hand and located the pulsating vein in the creature's back that she had seen before. She hesitated for only a moment, until Dad's advice about not putting off unpleasant things came to mind.

Here I go, Dad, she thought as she grabbed her wrist with her free hand and plunged the needle to the hilt in the bulging vein. She didn't wait to see what the monster would do or if it felt the needle before she pushed the plunger all the way in, emptying the insulin into the Feng. She finished without a moment to spare. Before she could pull the empty syringe from the monster, the Feng turned and wrenched the needle from her fingers.

Rrrrrraaaagggggggggffff! The Feng's angry roar sounded as though it had no business being anywhere near this beautiful wood, or anywhere else on earth. The monster whirled around and grabbed Hannah's wrists with its two front hands, then placed its dripping maw only inches from her face.

"*Prepare to recccceive your reward,*" the creature growled with a sneer.

The Feng lifted its head and opened its mouth, revealing rows of yellow, dripping teeth behind the tusk-like fangs. Hannah cringed and could do nothing more than turn her head so she wouldn't see the fangs as they plunged into her body. When she did so, her wavy brown hair with the three-dimensional fairy-blossom depiction of a tiger appeared to come alive. It turned its magnificent orange-and-white head directly at the Feng, reached out with a massive claw, and swatted at the monster's face.

"*Yaaaawwww!*" The Feng recoiled as if it had just touched its tongue to a hot stove, and for a moment, Hannah saw something new in the monster's black eyes: *fear.*

The moment passed, and the monster charged toward her, preparing to put an end to this nuisance with mysterious hair and voice that could cause it so much pain. Hannah closed her eyes and prayed, expecting to feel the plunge of the fangs at any moment.

Achwhoooooosh! Instead of the pain of the creature's fangs plunging into her flesh, Hannah felt the rush of putrid air past her face as if the monster had emptied its lungs on her. She opened her eyes to see a red-faced Feng turning to face the cliff. The cliff and . . .

"Dad!"

Hannah's father held a stick the size of a large baseball bat. Even with scratches all over his face and arms and a large rip down the side of his shirt, Dad looked better to Hannah than ever before. Dad lunged forward, swinging the stick over his head as if to give the Feng another pounding, but in mid-swing, he turned the stick toward Hannah. With a *crack!* the stick shattered the crusty webbing that trapped her feet.

"Now run, baby!" Dad turned to the Feng, placing himself between it and Hannah. "Run!" he called over his shoulder as the Feng attacked.

Hannah watched as Dad landed a solid blow right between the Feng's bulging eyes. The creature let out a roar and charged Dad, who moved away from Hannah, leading the Feng toward the bluff.

Hannah kicked the last of the shattered web chunks from her feet and took a quick look around. Her choices were clear. She could run down the hill, away from the raging battle between Dad and the Feng, or she could try to help. She made up her mind in an instant. She ran over to the tree imprisoning Misty and tried to yank the webbing off the wood sprite.

"My sword, Shaefrond," Misty said, gesturing to the foot of the tree.

Hannah picked up the golden sword and handed it to Misty, who used it to finish freeing herself from the webbing.

"Now, quickly," Misty said, "ask your father to lure the Feng to the cage. I must be in position if we are to have any chance."

Hannah called to Dad, who was battling the Feng at the edge of the bluff. "This way, Dad."

"Run, Hannah!" Dad was clearly confused and, judging by the way he was moving, was starting to tire.

"No, Dad." Hannah took a step closer to the fighting pair and waved him toward her. "Trust me."

Dad, for an instant, took his eyes off the Feng to look where Hannah was gesturing. The Feng saw its opportunity and took a swat at Dad's undefended head, but the blow was off mark and missed Dad by an inch. Hannah looked at the monster and saw the clear signs of low blood sugar: rapid breathing, sweat dripping from the monster's face, veins swollen and pulsating, indicating a fast heartbeat, and coordination that was off, making the fiend slower and less steady.

Yes! The insulin she'd injected in it seemed to be working, but the creature's strength was unaffected. One of the monster's fists aimed at Dad's face, missed, and shattered a sapling into pieces. The Feng was still very dangerous.

Hannah and Misty placed themselves in position at the open cage that now, thanks to Verple, was missing most of its leaf lid.

"Now remember, Shaefrond," Misty said, glancing at the battle raging at the edge of the bluff, "now that he knows about the trap, I have to stay below, where I can trip the lid if our plan is going to work. I will be unable to assist you."

Hannah nodded and caught Dad's eyes. His confusion was clear. She knew it wouldn't be long before he would not have the energy to avoid the Feng's blows. Without saying a word, Hannah opened her arms and motioned toward the trap at her feet.

Dad understood.

Using the last bit of his strength, he renewed his attack on the Feng. The monster, operating at half its normal speed, started to back up under Dad's repeated blows, until its back was only inches from the edge of the trap.

Hannah could see Dad had nothing left. The previous battle with the Feng, as well as the time he had spent as the monster's prisoner, had taken its toll. His arms drooped at his sides, and his breathing came in rapid huffs. The Feng, its eight legs shaking, propelled its dripping fangs at Dad's chest.

Dad attempted to dodge but was too late. The fangs raked across his chest, shredding his shirt and leaving two deep scratches. The effect of the poison was immediate. Dad collapsed in front of the trembling Feng.

The monster swiveled toward Hannah, who stood open-mouthed on the other side of the pit, not yet understanding what she'd just seen.

Dad had fallen.

CHAPTER 23

NOWHERE TO RUN

"You sssee, inssssect. Your kind isss nothing to meee." The Feng crept toward Hannah. It stopped, unaware that its shaking front legs hung over the edge of the trap. The creature stretched forward, placing its hideous face only inches from Hannah's. Sweat poured off its ugly face and down its legs, and the creature's black, smoky eyes seemed to have trouble focusing on her.

"I can sssummon othersss to do my wwwwill. I can tranccce my prey with my gazzze ssso they cannot move until they feeeel the sssting of my bite. I am immortal. I cannot diiiee..."

Hannah drifted off into a trance at the rhythmic sound of the creature's voice. Maybe the monster was right. Why try to fight it? It couldn't be killed. Misty had said so. It was immortal. She'd seen how it healed after it had been cut and bruised, leaving not so much as a scratch. It'd be much easier to just give up, wouldn't it?

Her eyes started to droop, and all she wanted to do was curl up in the leaves at her feet and take a long nap.

But something inside her told her to glance past the monster to where Dad lay still as death on the forest floor. Both his shoes were gone, and his pants were matted with dirt. His blue shirt was now a filthy brown and hung by frayed shreds from his shoulders. He had given everything trying to save his Sunshine.

The sight of him lying motionless on the forest floor lit something in the bottom of Hannah's chest. It was as if a switch had been flipped, chasing away the darkness of the Feng. At first, it was no brighter than a small nightlight, but it quickly grew until all darkness, sadness, and fear had been driven away.

As Hannah came back to the world, she heard the Feng still talking in its rhythmic chant. "—*bring me tribute. All willl know of my greatnesss, and you willll bow before meee and shhhall ssserve meee.*"

"No." Hannah's response was not loud, barely more than a whisper.

The creature leaned closer to her, twisting its ugly face more than she thought possible, and spat, *"You know not who I aaam! In all the world, there isss none like meee."*

Hannah looked directly at the smoky blackness of the monster's eyes and calmly said, "I am Hannah Biel, fiend, and in all the world, there is none like *me*."

The monster wrinkled its forehead and drew back, apparently confused by either Hannah's comment or her sudden lack of fear.

"I can kill with a ssscratch!" The Feng came closer, tilting its head back so Hannah could see all of the long fangs hanging out of its distorted face. One more step, and the monster would be directly over the trap. *"I can change my sssizzze to as big aaas a bear or aaas sssmall as a rrrat."*

"And I can brighten the cloudiest day with my smile." Hannah's eyes did not leave the monster's face, but her voice rose as she decided that no matter what happened, the monster could not change her essence, that thing that Misty had spoken of that made her *her*.

When this day was over, she would still be Hannah, Dad's Sunshine, Shaefrond to the Fey, and nothing this dark creature could do could change that. Her mind and her choices were still her own. As long as her choices were hers to make, she would make them without fear of what this foul beast would think or do to her. *Yes, that's better*, she thought, all fear like a balloon she'd released on a windy day. She could still feel it, but it was so small, it no longer bothered her.

"I can sweeten tea with a joke. I can chase away sickness with a laugh and melt sadness with a song. You don't scare me, monster. You're no more than a mosquito badly in need of a swatting!"

At this, the Feng let out a spit-filled roar and lunged for Hannah's throat, stepping directly on what was left of the trap's cover. In one *snap! the cover* gave way, and the monster disappeared from sight to the bottom of the pit.

"Now, Misty, now!" Hannah called.

Misty flipped the catch that would slam shut the lid of the cage. The Feng realized what was happening and stuck a hand between the lid and the edge of the cage in a desperate attempt to keep the lid from closing. Hannah jumped on top of the cage and bounced the Feng's fingers back into the cage.

On the last bounce, just as the last finger was slipping beneath the lid, Verple came dashing out from wherever he had been hiding and charged the finger.

"For Ash, Oak, and Birch!" Verple yelled, shouting the names of his three favorite taffy vats destroyed by the Feng when it had raided his village. Verple managed to get one swing of his sword on the finger before the lid slammed shut.

Misty wasted no time. "Stand back!" she called as she started the process that would transform the box. *Click, slide, snick!* and the box was half the size it had been a minute before. Each time the box was reduced in size, the Feng let go a roar of frustration and reduced its own size to match the box. Misty continued sliding, moving, and arranging the sides of the box until it was of a size that would easily fit into her bean pouch.

Just before Misty slipped the tiny box into her pouch, the Feng, now looking like a harmless wood spider with ridiculously large fangs, squeeked, *"Fear meee, girl, for one daaay, you will feeeel my sssting!"* The monster's voice faded as Misty dropped the cage into her pouch.

Before closing the top of her pouch, Misty pulled from it a handful of green leaves tied with a string. She handed the leaves to Hannah. "Grind these into a powder and sprinkle them into your father's mouth and in his wounds. Do this quickly, while there is still time."

Hannah did as Misty instructed while the wood sprite worked to free the Fey host from the sticky webs of the Feng.

CHAPTER 24

TRIBUTE

"You use this to choose colors that go best together." Misty held up the velvety, multicolored circle the size of a potato chip in the pile of presents at Hannah's feet. "The fairies use these to decide which flowers to plant and where to plant them. That way, they can be sure nothing clashes." At Hannah's raised eyebrow, Misty bent slightly at the waist and put her hands on her hips, pretending to scold Hannah. "You would not want to be walking in the wood, having meaningful thoughts of beauty and truth, and see a purple poppy mallow right next to a yellow marsh marigold, would you?"

"Eeewww!" The assembled Fey crooned at Misty's description as if they had all been sprayed by a skunk at the same time—all except the bog gnomes, who were having their own separate party some distance away from the rest of the Fey.

Hannah glanced in their direction to see Verple retelling the story of how *he* had captured the monster, to the *oohs* and *aahs* of his fellow gnomes.

Despite the festivities and the strange and beautiful gifts stacked at her feet, Hannah kept looking in the direction where Dad lay a few feet away. The Fey had piled soft loam under him several inches thick and had covered him with a silky red blanket woven from fox hair. He was sleeping peacefully, and his breathing was steady. The Fey healers had examined him and assured Hannah that he would be fine once he had rested and the last traces of the Feng's poison had been flushed from his system, but she was taking no chances. She would not lose Dad again.

". . .and this is Gethsemne tea."

Hannah's thoughts snapped back to Misty, who was continuing her description of the Fey gifts.

Misty held up a silver bag drawn at the top with a string. "When mixed with fresh beet juice and drunk in the light of a full moon, this rare herb will overcome serious illnesses."

Hannah froze. Why hadn't she thought of this before? The Fey were a strange and mysterious folk but old in tradition and wise in the ways of herbs and medicine. Surely, they would know how to cure her diabetes!

Hannah considered her gifts: a locket on a purple chain with a beautiful painting of the Missouri River at sunset, complete with moving water and changing seasons; a set of penny-sized disks that, when rubbed together once, would keep flies and mosquitoes away all day; a small brush that would imprint the image of birds, butterflies, rainbows, and such in her hair; and a bead on a short string that would, when hung around her ear, allow her to "pull strands from the tapestry" and weave them into her songs. When Hannah had asked Misty to explain this, Misty had just smiled with a wink and patted Hannah's leg with her tiny hand. "There is much I would show you if you care to learn," she had said. Then, as the Fey were in the habit of doing, she had changed the subject to talk about the chances of an early snow this year and whether crickets would be a problem in the fall.

The gifts were beautiful and unlike any Hannah had ever seen, but the dread of living with her disease shadowed even these wonderful treasures like a dark storm cloud threatening to ruin a picnic. As rare and valuable as these gifts were, she would trade them all to be rescued from her diabetes.

Hannah dropped to her knees so she could look Misty straight in the eye. "Misty Meadowatcher, I have a ques–"

Misty quickly raised her hand. "No, Shaefrond. The Gethsemne will not cure your diabetes." Misty's words, though gentle as a feather floating on a pond, hit Hannah like a ten-ton rock.

"I have asked the most skilled healers among us," Misty continued, "and am told there are herbs that may help you, but there is nothing they have found that will take this challenge from you."

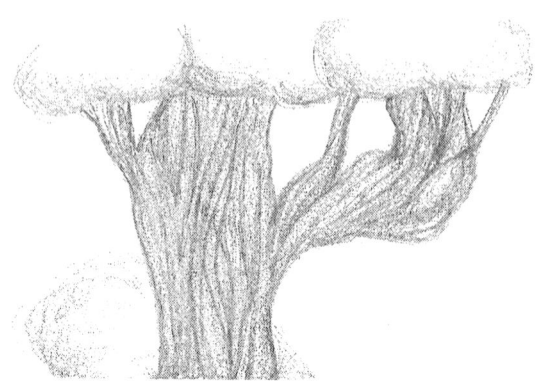

CHAPTER 25

THE DIMMENLARCH MESSAGE

Hannah buried her face in her hands and crumpled to the grass, feeling foolish for daring to believe for a moment there was an easy way out of this dreadful disease. The Fey, whether out of curiosity or respect, stopped their singing and dancing and sat in the short grass in the shadow of the old oak. Only the crackling of the tiny fires scattered throughout the clearing broke the silence of the quiet evening.

"Challenge!" Hannah cried. "You think this is just a challenge, like climbing a steep hill or singing a hard song? This is nothing like that!" Hannah got to her feet and stood with tears streaming down her face. The slight bend in her waist made the tears drop off her face and plop onto the dry leaves at Misty's feet.

"No, Shaefrond," Misty said softly. The wood sprite lightly stepped to Hannah's side. "It is nothing like climbing a steep hill or singing a hard song, but a challenge it is—one that, if overcome, will transform the beautiful, tender sprig of a girl you are now into a mighty champion with the strength of a spring storm and wisdom that will enrich your family for generations."

The crest of anger fell from her, and Hannah dropped again to her knees, shoulders slumped, feeling more tired than she could remember ever being before.

Misty gestured above their heads to the ancient oak tree that was five times older than any person Hannah knew. She could see the tree clearly in the bright light of the full moon. It was less than half the height of some of the healthy giants of its kind that were plentiful in the park. From the ground, it rose about six feet and then abruptly changed directions as if it had tried to escape being a tree when it was growing but had given up, then resigned itself to its lot in life. The trunk was marked by large gaping gashes, and the branches that grew from it were stunted and equally misshapen.

Misty walked to the base of the tree and gently touched its bark. "This tree is known as the Dimmenlarch. As you can see," Misty gestured up the length of the tree's twisted trunk, "the Dimmenlarch has been *challenged*."

Hannah wrapped her arms around her knees and remained silent. She and Dad had been here many times. The tree had been verified to be over 400 years old and, being the oldest in the state of Nebraska, was a local attraction.

"When I found it," Misty continued, "it was but a sapling and suffering from a rare disease that threatened to kill it unless I moved quickly. This disease will eat a plant from the inside out, and but for the Dimmenlarch, I am aware of no tree afflicted with it that has survived."

"So, what does that have to do with me?" Hannah asked.

"For seventeen summers, I battled with the disease that was trying to sever the life stream of the young tree. Finally, with the help of the woodland fairies, who have learned the songs that help such things grow, we were able to rid the

Dimmenlarch of the disease." Misty sat down in one of the gaping openings in the bark. "But the price was heavy.

"Many summers after restoring the tree, Faisle noticed there was something different about its wood. He had crafted a flute from one of its branches that had fallen from it after a storm. When played, the flute produced a note so pure, even the wind took notice. The oldest of us, even those who had lived among the Drucha, had never heard an instrument make such a clean and wholesome tone. It was as if the Dimmenlarch was thanking us."

"But it's just an old tree," Hannah said, a bit surprised.

"For centuries," Misty continued, "this *old tree*, the Dimmenlarch, has gifted us with its unique wood, allowing us to fashion instruments and tools that surpass any in the world. Fey from near and far come to this wood to behold the magnificence of the Dimmenlarch and barter for its gifts. You see?"

No, Hannah was not sure she did see.

Misty stepped forward and spread her arms as if she were carrying a large basket. "Great and wonderful things come from these challenges. Whether it be the Dimmenlarch, the fairy, Feyla, or your queen of beauty, none of these did great things *in spite of* their challenges." Misty stepped even closer to Hannah. "No, they did them only *because* of their challenges."

"You act as though diabetes is a gift!" Hannah felt the tears starting to rise again.

"No, Shaefrond. A magnificent gift there is, but it is not the diabetes. It is the gift of freewill that is bestowed on you every day when you are faced with the choice."

"What choice?" Hannah asked through gritted teeth.

"The choice between overcoming your challenge and living, or permitting it to overcome you. Each day you choose to live, you are growing a new branch on your tree. Choose well consistently, and your branches and roots will grow so strong and so deep, they will withstand any storm, any hardship. You will achieve wisdom that others will never know—wisdom that only comes to one who has conquered a great foe. You will be an example to others who will see your strength and draw goodness, understanding, and peace from it. In this, Shaefrond, you will gift others."

Misty climbed the Dimmenlarch and stood in another gap in the ancient bark, so her eyes were even with Hannah's. "So you see, my friend, a great gift it is, this freewill of yours, and now you must decide how you will use it."

"I think I'm beginning to see," Hannah said.

Misty glanced in the direction where Hannah's father was sleeping. "I must leave you now." In one graceful spring, she landed in the leaves at Hannah's feet, where she tucked one hand at her waist and bowed low. "I am truly thankful for having met you, Hannah Biel, champion and beloved friend of the Fey. Forget not what you have learned here, and it will serve you well. Let no person be lessened from having met you. Leave a piece of yourself in all that you do, and be grateful for your mistakes, for as teachers, they have no equal. Take joy in simplicity and satisfaction in knowing that wisdom is found in the most unlikely of places. Fare you well, friend." Misty turned and headed across the clearing, which was now empty except for Priscilla and a few staggering bog gnomes.

"Misty," Hannah called as the nimble wood sprite walked toward the edge of the clearing, "will I see you again?"

Misty stopped, turned, and said with a smile in her voice the size of the sun, "Of course." She started back toward the forest. Before she disappeared into the undergrowth, she turned and pointed to one of the gaps in the Dimmenlarch. "If you leave a message there, we can keep in touch between lessons."

"Lessons?" Hannah asked.

"Oh yes," Misty said with an even bigger smile. "Did I not tell you I had much to show you?" And with a wave of her hand, Misty Meadowatcher, wood sprite guardian of Ponca State Park, vanished into the forest.

*   *   *

"Hannah? Baby, is that you?" Dad staggered around the Dimmenlarch, leaning on the old tree for support.

"Dad!" Hannah yelped as she sprung toward him and hugged him around the waist. The two clutched each other like they would never let go. Dad whispered his apologies and his promises into Hannah's ear.

After several minutes, Dad let go and looked Hannah over, checking for injuries. He stopped when he saw the tiger in her hair but said nothing. Finally, finding only a few scrapes and bruises, he gazed at her with a mixed look of relief and confusion. "I thought I'd lost you, baby. How did you get away from that . . . that monster?"

Before she could answer, a giant burp erupted from one of the three remaining bog gnomes who had not yet made it to the edge of the clearing. Even though the full moon lit the clearing well, Dad could not see what had made the obnoxious noise. He peered here and there until Hannah gathered her gifts in the fox-hair blanket, wrapped her arm around his waist, and pointed him toward the trail that led to the road.

"Let's go home, Dad. I'm hungry, and it's story night." Then with a wink, she added, "I'll tell the one tonight, if you don't mind."

Acknowledgments

Friendship is unnecessary, like philosophy, like art.
. . . It has no survival value; rather it is one of those things which give value to survival.

—C. S. Lewis

As Lewis did with survival, I would classify contributors to this work in two ways: the **Necessaries**, those without whose contribution the story would have never been told outside the bedrooms of my children, and the **Sparklers**, those who came along later who gave the work color, flavor, and sparkle.

My sincere and deepest thanks to the **Necessaries**, most notably Steve Davern and Sue Headley, who saw the path I would walk in these pages sooner and more clearly than I.

I am no less grateful to the **Sparklers**, who, through their inspiration and thoughtful critique, gave the work order, flavor, and a thorough scrubbing where scrubbing was needed: Jacqueline Horsfall, Melissa Tucker, Peter Lord, Gary Newman, Jeff Fields, and the staff of Ponca State Park, who never seemed to tire of me.

My special thanks to my wife, Karen, and our children Laikyn (whose art adorns the chapter headings), Braelie, Bella, Blaeden, and Edyn for giving me a reason to write and for showing me where the magic hides.

About the Author

Blane Brummond lives in Ponca, Nebraska, with his wife and five children. Blane grew up in South Dakota across the mile-wide Missouri River from Ponca State Park, where he spent many sunny summer afternoons gazing at the bluffs on the far shore, imagining what secrets the dark and beautiful wood held.

After he was diagnosed with juvenile diabetes at the age of twenty-five, Blane was faced with the choices faced by thousands of young people every year: whether to and how hard to fight the disease. As a veteran of the elite US Army Airborne Rangers, surrender was not an option. He would fight. Blane pushed forward, graduating from college and then law school. He participated in a host of physically demanding activities such as college wrestling, skydiving, mountain biking, Kung Fu, and one professional MMA cage match. He enjoys studying Christian apologetics, writing music, and hosting an annual fairy hunt that has attracted seekers from as far away as Chicago.

Hannah is Blane's debut novella. The book grew out of the tales he'd been telling his four girls of a beautiful wood sprite he'd met who had a fondness for mushrooms and good manners. On one occasion, the wood sprite had actually given him a map of one of her mushroom farms and her permission to harvest her crop. The map was followed, the mushrooms were found, and sweet memories were sewn into the minds of all.

The book was also born of the author's desire to give hope, support, and encouragement to the thousands of children diagnosed with juvenile diabetes every year—13,000 in the United States alone—and understanding to those touched by the disease through friends or relatives. Tragically, the disease is usually diagnosed at an age when the child's self-image is still forming and when fitting in is more important than just about anything else. *Hannah* is Blane's attempt to show these children, or any other child who doesn't fit the norm, that being kind is better than being popular, that physical strength is no match for strength of character, and that a person's value has absolutely nothing to do with what classmates think of them.

CPSIA information can be obtained
at www.ICGtesting.com
Printed in the USA
FFOW01n1317300814

Winds of the Rio Grande

Journey up the wild and raging river

Francis Louis Guy Smith

Winds of the Rio Grande

Journey up the wild and raging river

Copyright © 2011 Books by guy

All rights reserved.

ISBN: 978-1466340787